The ago[n

Carl Lyons kne[   ]ken.
He'd seen craz[   ]?

He relaxed his [   ]ack, slid his handcuffed
wrists beneath him, then pulled up with all his
strength. The pain became a white light.

The handcuffs broke. Screaming like a beast, he
slammed his numb arms against the heads of his
captors. Blood splashed onto the car's windows.

The Ford sedan swerved out of control. It leaped
the curb.

Lyons fell backward from the open door and rolled
onto the sidewalk. Faces peered down at him.

"Get back!" roared Lyons, aiming a .38 at the car.
"Stand back! Back!"

Two kids gaped at him, then at each other. "That
cop's all messed up. Betcha he dies...."

Tower of Terror

Don Pendleton & Dick Stivers

A GOLD EAGLE BOOK FROM

TORONTO · NEW YORK · LOS ANGELES · LONDON

First edition June 1982
Second printing August 1982
Third printing December 1982
First published in Australia March 1984

ISBN 0-373-61201-X

Special thanks and acknowledgment to
L. R. Payne for his contributions to this work.

Printed in Australia by
The Dominion Press–Hedges & Bell, Victoria 3130.

Our democracy won its independence
through the heroism and sacrifice
of countless citizen warriors—some
recognized by history, others anonymous.
Now we are threatened by terror.
At any time, without warning,
despite the efforts of our police and
armed forces, the defence of family or
friends could fall on the individual. To
these citizens, who may suddenly find
themselves warriors, we dedicate this book.

Carl Lyons: blond blue-eyed ex-LAPD sergeant, this recent veteran of the Justice Department's war against organized crime has seen enough blow-torched, pliers-mangled corpses to know what to do about today's psycho punks—shoot first.

Rosario Blancanales: from a Chicano background, he's known as Pol for Politician. Able Team's broad-shouldered senior member now fights the war against international terrorism with a special kind of sophistication and fury.

Herman Schwarz: code-named Gadgets for his wizardry with electronic devices, this Vietnam vet with metaphysical leanings has a genius-level IQ and a penchant for the unusual and unexpected in strategy and action.

Eight persons die in bombing of bus

NEW YORK (Special)—Six passengers, a tour guide and a bus driver were killed instantly today in the bomb-blasting of a sight-seeing bus in midtown Manhattan.

Police investigators at the scene within minutes of the tragic occurrence said the blast was caused by a plastic-explosive bomb that was probably in excess of 50 pounds. Debris from the destroyed vehicle was found over a two-block area.

Names of the victims, whose identification was virtually impossible, have been withheld until notification of next-of-kin.

The bombing was claimed by the FALN in a telephoned message to the mayor's office. The terrorist-group message, recorded automatically at City Hall, said:

"Las Fuerzas Armadas de Liberación Nacional denounces the imperial fascist regime of the United States of America. No longer will we plead for justice and liberty. No longer will your corporations profit from the slavery of our people. No longer will Yankees live in comfort while our people live in misery.

"We struck today to revenge the torture and murder of our comrades. We will strike tomorrow. We will make war on New York City until the United States liberates Puerto Rico.

"Viva Puerto Rico libre!"

Police said the voice recorded on City Hall tapes had been "electronically neutralized" to prevent voice-graph identification.

The New York Police Department's elite Anti-Terrorist Unit said there was no connection between today's bombing and a predawn gas-main explosion yesterday in lower Manhattan that destroyed a cafeteria and several shops. There were no injuries in yesterday's mishap.

Destruction of

CLASSIFIED: TOP SECRET

OPERATIONAL IMMEDIATE

FR WHITE HOUSE/BROGNOLA
TO ABLE TEAM

MISSION ALERT X
EXERCISE FULL PREROGATIVES X
TOPMAN REQUESTS X
RE NEW YORK BOMBINGS
NYPD/FBI INFORMANTS IN FALN REPORT NO
EVIDENCE FALN INVOLVEMENT IN BOMBINGS X
MICROSCOPIC/CHEMICAL ANALYSIS OF EXPLOSIVES
COMPLETE X AMERICAN C-4 X CAPTURED REPUBLIC
OF VIETNAM 1975 X ANALYSIS OF VOICEPRINT
INDICATES USE OF ELECTRONIC DEVICE OF
UNKNOWN DESIGN X UNKNOWN ORIGIN X NYPD
COOPERATING WITH FBI MISINFORMATION TO MEDIA
X DISCOVERY OF OTHER BOMBS SUPPRESSED X NO
MEDIA X FBI/DEFENSE DEPT/TOPMAN SUSPECT
FOREIGN NATION SUPPLIED EXPLOSIVES X VIETNAM
TO CUBA TO USA X NYPD/FBI INVESTIGATION
CONTINUES X TOPMAN REQUESTS ABLE TEAM BREAK
FOREIGN CONNECTION X IDENTIFY TERRORIST
GROUP X CAPTURE/LIQUIDATE X FULL
LOGISTICS/RESOURCES

CLASSIFIED: TOP SECRET

OPERATIONAL IMMEDIATE

FR STONYMAN ONE
TO BROGNOLA/ABLE TEAM/STONY OPS

STONYMAN ONE SENDS FR ANKARA X RE NEW YORK
BOMBINGS X ABLE TEAM ASSIGNMENTS X LYONS TO
LEAD ABLE TEAM X LEAD LIAISON NYPD/FBI/CIA X
BLANCANALES LIAISON ALL PUERTO RICAN/CUBAN
INTELLIGENCE X SCHWARZ COORDINATE
ELECTRONIC INTELLIGENCE X GOOD LUCK X WISH I
WAS THERE X BT

PROLOGUE

It had been a dream of Mack Bolan's for many years. It was a dream of hope and a dream of despair.

Sometimes it was a real dream, a vision in the deepest sleep, that the Executioner's Death Squad—a hellish unit of ruthless, disillusioned veterans of Vietnam—was reborn in glory from the flames and ashes. More often it was a daydream that the guys were back again, the warriors of Death Squad on the attack in the world once more.

Death Squad. They were certainly not an hallucination. They were once a maelstrom of nine very real and extremely dangerous men. They were heroes of the Vietnam War. They were recruited by Mack Bolan when the Black Hand let out a $100,000 contract on the big guy's life.

What a unit! Chopper Fontanelli and Deadeye Washington...Flower Child Andromede and Gunsmoke Harrington...Boom-Boom Hoffower... Bloodbrother Loudelk...Whispering Zitka...and Politician Blancanales and Gadgets Schwarz.

All but the last two were killed, mercilessly felled by Mafia guns in the Executioner's final wipeout strike against the mob's hardsite on the cliffs of Balboa, Southern California.

The Executioner himself was wounded in that engagement. And the bloodied survivors, Pol and Gadgets, were captured by police in a retreat from the Beverly Hills estate of LA czar Julian DiGeorge. The best thing about that bitter time was Carl Lyons, a sergeant with the LAPD, who became a Bolan ally, later joined him in his campaigns in San Diego, Las Vegas, Hawaii.

After the carnage in California, Bolan vowed never to involve allies in what he saw as an exclusively personal crusade.

But it is hard to keep good men down, especially those hardasses who had no fear of death and remained undaunted by any Mafia.

Blancanales and Schwarz and Lyons had in fact found new strength in Bolan's cauldron of justice and retribution, and they would remain allies of the man in black to the fullest extent of his final miles. For them, there was no other choice.

Carl Lyons was the only one of the three who had been baptized in fires other than the Asian war. His experience was with the Los Angeles police, a career which reached its brutal limits with the get-Bolan detail codenamed "Hardcase," a war waged against the Executioner by law-enforcement officers because of Bolan's severe infractions of the law in his own war against the Syndicate. It was a fierce assignment, and it involved Lyons' growing awareness that Bolan was right at whatever cost. A new road was opening up for him. It was the road of righteous war, paved by that giant American who *lived large*. For Lyons, a trim blue-eyed man of iron who knew the ways of unconventional combat as well as any veteran, there would be no turning back.

Rosario 'Pol' Blancanales was a Black Beret in 'Nam, and served on the infamous Long Range Reconnaissance Patrols. It was as a guide on penetration missions in that conflict that Pol first met Mack Bolan. Blancanales earned his "politician" nickname from his skills in dealing with all types of people, his ability to win acceptance easily and blend chameleon-like into any environment. During the Vietnam pacification programs he learned the obscure dialects of the country fluently; it was an unusual accomplishment, indicative of high intelligence as well as his outstanding degree of ordinary common sense.

Herman "Gadgets" Schwarz was the wizard, a counter-intelligence advisor in Vietnam who had turned his genius-level skills at electronics to good effect in the Death Squad. Seeing Gadgets blaze away with a primed Ingram, it was hard to visualize him as the person he really was—the favorite son of a reclusive, slightly screwball lady in Pasadena who filled her house with cats and Herman's leftover gadgetry. But nothing was predictable about Schwarz.

Nothing was predictable about any of these individuals: seasoned in guerilla war of the utmost extremes, they operated now in a nation stalked by multinational terrorists, fighting an undeclared war much more momentous than anything that had gone before.

Two of them—Pol and Gadgets—had started a detective agency called the Able Group, which with Blancanales' sister Toni soon became a multioperative team that took on cases too involved to be cracked by ordinary law enforcement. Meanwhile

Lyons had become a Federal Agent, an undercover specialist for the Justice Department.

These roles would soon lead to the realization of Bolan's dream of rebirth. His John Phoenix program, a war for the Executioner that would take him to new shores and new enemies, had left the home flank dangerously exposed. And so the Stony Man team was forged, a grouping of powerful individuals headquartered in the secrecy of Stony Man Farm, which was their heavily equipped hardsite in Virginia's Shenandoah Valley. Historically the scene of a four-year "valley of humiliation" for the Union forces against Stonewall Jackson, it became a fitting locale for the ultimate rebellion: Death Squad is back!

It has always been Mack Bolan's feeling that the universe is a violent thing, created by a series of explosions. Bolan and his allies are those continuing explosive forces that sustain and advance life itself. None of them will ever really be on stand-by—they are always in action.

Now named Able Team, Mack's three-man anti-terrorist operation will move into action whenever conventional forces are unable to act. It is Able Team's job to take over from law enforcement when the odds are too stacked. That bright, crisp morning in New York City, for example, when something gross and bloody happened in Wall Street...a day and night that were to be slashed and torn with terror. Who would have thought that the whole thing began in Florida, in Miami's not-very-crisp, far from morning-bright "Little Havana"? Able Team would soon find out...

Backed by a brilliant Stony Man unit that includes Hal Brognola and April Rose, the Executioner's Able Team is a dream come true. Born in flames, they are ready to die at any time, but they will never be extinguished.

Come in, Able.

1

They followed Rosario Blancanales through the crowded, neon-bright streets of Miami's "Little Havana," never getting too close, but never letting Blancanales out of sight. The Latin nightlife of the district moved around them, young women in tight skirts, macho young men in disco finery, the groups of big-bellied older men standing in front of cafés, laughing.

Carl Lyons leaned across the front seat of the van and adjusted the passenger-side rearview mirror. The nightlife didn't fool him. Many of those macho young men trained in the Florida Everglades, grunting through swampwater as their instructors fired machine-gun bursts to keep their heads down. Those older fellows, who looked like grandfathers, were cold killers. Betrayed at the Bay of Pigs, some of them financed their dreams of recapturing Cuba through the smuggling and sale of cocaine, heroin, and marijuana. If any of them was to learn the identity of Rosario Blancanales, or see into the interior of the closed van carrying Carl Lyons and Herman "Gadgets" Schwarz, there would be death. The FBI had lost several agents in the streets and alleys of Little Havana. The agents simply disappeared.

We're searching for explosives, not drugs, Lyons

thought. *But we'd never get the chance to explain.*

Blancanales stood a few car lengths behind the van, talking with a fat man in a polyester leisure suit named Hector. Lyons watched them in the rearview mirror.

"What're they talking about?" Lyons called back to Gadgets.

"Hector's got the information," Gadgets answered from behind the curtain that screened him from view. In the back of the van, Gadgets monitored the body-transmitter that Blancanales wore. Every word he spoke and almost all of Hector's words were transmitted to the van. A tape machine recorded the dialogue. Gadgets also maintained communication with the FBI Emergency Task Force assisting Able Team.

"How's the Politician making out?"

"Okay, I think. Wish my Spanish was better, those guys are talking real fast. And it's Cuban Spanish, so I don't know what I'm hearing—this is it! Hector says he's going to make a call. He has to make a phone call."

Lyons watched the man step to a pay phone, dial a number. Blancanales glanced down the street to the van. Lyons touched the brake pedal twice: flash–flash.

"Rosario's talking to me," Gadgets told him. "Everything's cool. It might be a go."

"Wish there was some way we could talk back." Lyons didn't like Blancanales being on one-way contact only.

"He's got it under control, he didn't need our

back-talk," Gadgets smiled. "Hey, the man's returned."

Lyons watched Blancanales and Hector cross the street. They got into a Cadillac. "Where are they going?"

"Hector says he'll take Rosario to the man who's got the information. It'll cost him a thousand dollars."

"I don't like it."

"*No bueno* is correct. Price is right, but what's with the car ride?"

"Gadgets, you come up front. You drive in case I have to jump."

"Be cool, Lyons. If the Politician's going along, he must feel okay about it. We'll just wing it."

"But I don't feel good about it. Getting in the man's car could be a quick ride to a hole in the ground. Pass me the Ingram and a couple of mags. Leave the gun in the wrapper."

Lyons wore a .357 magnum in a shoulder holster. But he believed in choosing the right tool for the job: a rifle with a scope for long shots; a pistol for tight shots; and when needed, a weapon for the middle range, which in this case was a silenced Ingram machine-pistol, requisitioned from the CIA arsenal.

Gadgets passed the plastic-wrapped weapon through the curtain. Then two extra magazines, thirty 9mm rounds each. As Lyons followed Hector's Cadillac through the Miami streets, he checked the silencer's mounting and jacked a round into the chamber. He flipped on the safety.

"What's going on with Anders?" he asked Gadgets.

"Keeping his distance. You want to talk to him?"

"Yeah."

Mitch Anders headed the Emergency Task Force. They worked in cooperation with the Able Team, providing back-up assistance whenever needed. But right now, Lyons didn't want assistance. Gadgets passed a hand-radio to Lyons, who spoke in double-talk code. "Politician's with the man. We're winging it. You stay away."

"Got it," Anders answered. "Two blocks away, minimum."

Lyons followed the Cadillac into a run-down area of warehouses and industrial buildings. The streets were empty except for parked semis and trailers. Lyons flicked off the van's lights, stayed a block behind the Cadillac. When it stopped, the ex-LAPD cop parked the van behind a truck.

"What now?" he asked Gadgets.

"Hector's saying his friend lives above the warehouse. They'll go up and talk to him."

"It's a trap! Stay with the van, I'm on my way." Lyons grabbed the Ingram from the floor.

"Wait! Rosario's got him. Lyons!"

"What?"

"Rosario's got him, says for you to come on up." Gadgets laughed. "Can't trick El Politico. He knows an ambush when it's in front of him."

"Let me have two hand-sets."

With the Ingram and the small hand-radios, Lyons ran to the doorway where Blancanales held the small, plump man up against the wall.

"What's happening, man?" Lyons put one of the radios into Blancanales' free hand.

"He and his friends were going to take me, ask me about my questions." Blancanales put a 9mm double-action Browning against Hector's throat, just an inch above the bright pinks and blues of his floral-print shirt. "I think he was going to sell me to the man I wanted to ask about."

Lyons stripped the plastic bag off the silenced machine-pistol, scanned the alleys and doorways near them. Blancanales questioned Hector in rapid-fire Spanish, prodding him with the Browning. Hector answered, cringing.

"When we walk in there," Blancanales indicated the door to the warehouse, "they'll take me. Hector's friends."

"Is there another way in?"

Hector answered in English. "Through the back."

"You take us in there," Lyons told Hector, pointing at him with the Ingram. "If you want to live, you take us in quiet, we ask our questions, and then we leave. No one gets hurt. We'll even pay the thousand dollars. What do you want to do?"

"The man you wish to question is not here. I have not seen him since I sold him the ship. But I can tell you he does not smuggle drugs. He says he does, but he does not...."

There was the sound of shots in the building. Hector froze.

"What's going on?" Lyons demanded.

"I don't know," Hector answered, "but my son is in there." He looked in panic at Lyons and Blancanales. "My son knows more about this man that you want. Maybe he can answer your questions!"

"Lead the way," Lyons ordered.

They ran through a passageway sparkling with broken glass, stinking of urine, Hector slightly ahead, the well-built, light-footed Lyons and dark Blancanales following. There were more shots inside.

In the alley behind the buildings, there were three cars—two new Cadillacs and a year-old Lincoln. Though plump and over fifty, Hector moved fast, dodged between the cars. A form stepped from the shadows. Hector threw himself down as a shotgun blast smashed the Lincoln's hood.

Zipppp! Lyons's Ingram ripped the man like a silent chainsaw. Hector ran to the corpse, took its shotgun. Lyons was one step behind him. He pressed the still-smoking Ingram to Hector's head.

Hector didn't pause as he searched the dead man's pockets, took out 12-gauge shotgun shells. "Help me now, and I will tell my son to answer all your questions."

"Your word?" Lyons glared.

"You have my word." Hector smiled, loaded the 12-gauge. *"Amigos."*

"Por un momento," Blancanales added.

Hector threw open a steel door, sprinted into the dim interior of the warehouse. Shots flashed. There was a burst from an M-16.

Lyons called for assistance on his hand-set. "Anders! Lyons here. Time to move. Firefight in progress in a warehouse. Gadgets is out front. Repeat, firefight. Automatic weapons. Seal the area. We will attempt to capture suspects for interrogation."

"Moving," Anders' voice responded from the hand-set. "We are approximately one minute away."

Lyons rolled through the doorway and took cover behind a fork lift. An automatic's burst punched into the concrete-block wall behind him. Blancanales ran past him, took cover in a high stack of crates.

Boxes and bales stacked on steel racks formed thick walls twelve feet high. Aisles as wide as a fork lift ran the length and width of the building. A dim exit light revealed a dead man near the door to the alley. He had taken a shotgun blast in the face. Most of his head was gone.

"Hector!" Lyons called out. "Where are you? Who's on your side? Which ones are the enemy?"

"Here!" Hector shouted from the far side of the warehouse. Shots echoed, the heavy blast of the shotgun, the ripping sound of the M-16. There were the pops of pistols. Then the blast of the shotgun again.

Hector ran toward them. He half carried a young Latino, about twenty years old. Blancanales braced his pistol hand with his other hand, fired round after round over their heads, into the shadows behind them.

Lyons saw someone move in another aisle. He saw the silhouette of an M-16 in a man's hand.

"Freeze!" Lyons shouted.

The man spun, but before he could aim the M-16, a stream of slugs ripped through his chest, spraying blood behind him. He was dead before he fell.

Hector gave the shotgun to Blancanales, eased his son to the floor. The boy's clothes were drenched with blood from two superficial wounds.

"I killed one of them. My son says there is only one other...."

"With the M-16? He's dead."

"And there is a friend of my son's back there, wounded very badly."

"A doctor's on the way," Lyons told him. "Now the answers."

In minutes, the alley and filthy streets around the warehouse looked like an FBI parking lot. But by that time, Able Team already had information that was to send them out of Miami, and far to the North.

2

Through the Starlite scope, its electronics turning the moonless night into day, Lyons watched them unload explosives.

Two men standing in the motor launch lifted each case by its rope handles, swung it onto the floating dock. The cases were wide and flat, too heavy for the man on the dock to carry. He dragged the cases one after another into the boathouse, then ran back for the next one. At the far end of the boathouse, a fourth man crouched against the wall, his M-16 pointed at the silent fields and marshes of the North Carolina coast. In the distance, more than a mile from the stagnant inlet, were brush-covered foothills, then forest. There were no lights, no highways, only the dirt road cutting through the salt marshes.

Lyons checked the safety on his rifle. He wanted no accident. This was not an ambush. If it had been, the four men would have been dead the moment the boat touched the dock. Quick as counting one, two, three, four. But Lyons was well aware that killing these four would not stop the terrorists in New York City.

He took his eye from the eyepiece, half turned to glance behind him. No headlights approaching. At some time during the night, however, a truck would come for those crates.

On the launch, the men stopped. Lyons watched one of them light a cigarette. Through the scope, the match flare looked like a spotlight on the man's face. The muffled engine started, and the launch chugged away. Only the man on the dock and the guard with the M-16 remained.

His radio hand-set clicked twice. Lyons acknowledged Blancanales' signal with a single click. He couldn't chance any words. Blancanales hid somewhere near the dock, his night-suited and black-faced form invisible in the tall weeds. The clicks to Lyons meant he was ready and waiting. And with luck....

Forget luck, Lyons told himself. Organization, discipline and patience: Lyons repeated the words as he searched the night for headlights. It wasn't luck that got us to this boathouse.

Back in Miami, Hector and his son Alfonso had confessed in the aftermath of the firefight that they had sold a rusting freighter to a smuggler running dope from the Caribbean to the United States. But the smuggler was unknown to the international drug gangs. Until the deal blew up in his face, Hector had thought the operation was a Federal scam to trap big-time dealers. Alfonso told him he had overheard a crewman say "Carolina."

This information had prompted Gadgets to focus his wizardry on the part of the Carolina coast where they were now encamped. He had electronically located a high-powered transmitter in this area, which was in communication with both New York City and a freighter off the coast, presumably the smugglers'.

In pinpointing the location of the transmitter, he had intercepted a coded message from the freighter to the boathouse. Though they couldn't break the code, the Able Team hoped it meant a delivery.

Lyons and Blancanales had waited near the coastline until dark, then hiked two miles through the marshes and fields, crawling the last few hundred yards. Gadgets stayed at the motel command center to monitor the frequencies for any communications.

In the field, Lyons took a position on a sandbank where he could watch both the boathouse and the road. Blancanales took a forward position where he would have cover from gunfire, but still be within a few steps of the dock. When the truck came to carry those crates of explosives to New York City, they would try to take the terrorists alive for interrogation. At least one of them.

Assuming the men in the boathouse were *members of the terrorist group,* Lyons thought. *Assuming there* was *plastic explosive in the crates. If we've gone to all this trouble just to grab some dopers....*

The blast stunned him like a hammer-blow to his head. Lyons instinctively covered himself as the rising fireball spewed bits and pieces of debris into the sky. It took him only a second to realize that the boathouse was gone.

"Rosario!" Lyons shouted. He ran to where the boathouse had been, thrashed through the tall weeds. "Rosario! You still here? You alive?"

The weeds burned in a dozen places, smoke swirling around Lyons as he searched for his friend. He found Blancanales sprawled behind a low mound near the water's edge. He was only semi-conscious, bleeding from a scalp wound.

Lyons dragged him a hundred yards along the edge of the inlet. It had been a big explosion, maybe a hundred pounds of C-4, but that accounted for only one of the crates the men had unloaded. He found an embankment that would protect them if any more of the explosives went off. He gently put Blancanales down.

"Hey, Rosario. Can you hear me?"

Blancanales looked at him, grinned. He ran his hand across his forehead, gauging the amount of blood, and said nothing.

"Don't sweat it, Politician. Your brains are still in your head. Can you hear?"

"Sort of." Blancanales tried to sit up, groaned, lay back. "Ohhhh, do I hurt." He closed his eyes, then very slowly sat up. "Something went wrong, didn't it?"

Flames lit the sky. "Yeah, and now we know what they had in those boxes, don't we?" smiled Lyons. "I've heard of high-powered dope, but this is ridiculous."

Blancanales glanced over the top of the embankment and surveyed the scene. "We get one good break, and now it's back to zero."

"Don't knock our luck, Rosario. At least you're alive."

An FBI helicopter shuttled them back to the ocean-front motel on the outskirts of a small town, hovering for a moment while Lyons and Blancanales carefully jumped the few feet to the sand on the dark beach. Then the chopper roared up and away, returning to the scene of the blast where teams of Federal agents searched the ashes.

They crossed the deserted beach to Mitch Anders' improvised office. His Emergency Task Force had commandeered the motel's twenty rooms.

"What happened out there?" Anders asked sternly. At two-thirty in the morning, he was freshly shaved and cologned and wore a three-piece suit.

Mud from the inlet's banks caked both Lyons and Blancanales. The blood from Blancanales' forehead ran down his face, mixing with the mud. They didn't answer immediately. Lyons eased himself into the cushions of the motel-modern chair, closed his eyes. He hadn't slept in three days.

"Well, I don't really know," Lyons said. "One second these four men were there, and the next, they weren't."

Anders looked to Blancanales. "What's the truth?"

"That was it. One of them was in the boathouse. He called the other one in. Then it was all over." Blancanales went to the room's sink and put his head under the faucet.

"You need a doctor?" Anders dialed a telephone number.

"Forget the doctor," Blancanales told him. "It's nothing."

Anders slammed down the phone. "So there was no shooting? What was it, a double suicide?"

Lyons laughed. "Must've been."

Anders ignored Lyons. "How'd you get that

wound, Blancanales? Couldn't you cowboys hold off? You had to take them?''

"Anders," Lyons protested. "don't give us the third degree."

"Don't give me your crap!"

"We weren't even *there*. How's that for a report? Does that answer your questions?''

"You have seriously jeopardized the progress of this investigation with your actions. It was over my objections that Commander Brognola assigned your team to this investigation. I will immediately...."

"This is the fact," Lyons interrupted. "We do not know what happened. We were in our positions, waiting for the truck. El Politico there is one very lucky man. If he'd just happened to have his head up at that moment, he would've lost it. You think we'd have made any kind of stupid move? He's lying there, maybe thirty-five, forty feet from a thousand pounds of plastic explosive. By some miracle, only about a hundred pounds went off...."

"All right!" Anders cut him off. "Thank you. I just wanted a report. You must understand my concern. Your team has methods that are quite different than those the Bureau would employ...."

"And the Bureau didn't come up with much, did they?" Lyons said. "A week and a half you're on it, and we're the ones who—''

"Gentlemen," Blancanales interrupted, "we're still on the same side. This is a team effort."

"Okay," Lyons agreed. "Us against them. Sorry I shot my mouth off, Anders."

"I hoped tonight would be the turning point,"

Anders sighed. "Well, I'm waiting on a call from the Coast Guard. They're taking the freighter, maybe they'll get someone for us."

There was a quick knock at the door. Gadgets Schwarz came in. "The shouting over?"

"Oh, yeah." Lyons stood. "We're just leaving. You get anything interesting, Gadgets?"

"Man, you cannot believe how interesting."

"On the accident?"

"Guess again, Lyons," Gadgets told him. "That big boom was no accident."

They crowded into Gadgets' motel room. Electronic gear—consoles, modules, racks of circuitry interlocked with receivers and tape machines—left space only for Gadgets' chair. Tools and cables and components covered the bed. A bundle of thick wires ran out the window to the temporary antennas hanging in the trees. Lyons pushed the cables aside, sat on the windowsill.

"I got it all. Listen." Gadgets ran tapes as he briefed them. "Here's the static of the launch engine, then your hand-sets clicking back and forth. . . ."

"Could they have picked up the walkie-talkies?" Anders asked. "When Lyons and Blancanales. . . ."

"Take it easy," Gadgets grinned. "Don't get paranoid. Just because I can, doesn't mean they can. Listen." Gadgets accelerated the tape, slowed it. "Here's the coded message, probably to New York. They had to send it twice before they got their confirmation. Hear it?"

A series of pulses came from the monitor speakers.

There was a pause, then the pulses repeated. Then a return pulse answered the code.

"That's their confirmation. Now a minute or two later, this voice comes on in the clear. It breaks in on their frequency. No code, no double talk, no scrambler."

It was in Castilian Spanish: "Please call in your comrade. It is imperative I immediately issue instructions to both of you."

"My Spanish isn't so good," Gadgets said. "So I had one of your Feds check it, Anders. It was just straight talk."

"Make a copy of that," Anders told him. "We'll want a voice graph."

"You got it already." Gadgets found a cassette in the clutter, tossed it to Anders.

"Play that voice again," Blancanales said. "Normal speed."

Gadgets backed up the tape, replayed it. Blancanales listened intently.

"That's correct Spanish," he commented. "Formal Spanish, like at a university."

Anders made a note on the cassette's label. "I'll have the linguists listen to it."

"Now listen to *this*." Gadgets slowed the playback of another part of the tape to half speed. Unnaturally slow voices slurred from the speakers. Then there was a jolt of electronic noise.

"That's when they died." Gadgets backed up the tape, played the single sound again. "That was a signal to a radio-command detonator. He blew away his own people."

"Are you absolutely certain?" Anders asked.

"Ab-so-loot-ly! I've made those things. The straight talk that breaks in is to make sure that they're using the frequency, so they'll be open to the detonating signal."

Anders turned to Lyons. "What do you think about this? How does it relate to their operation in New York?"

Lyons stood, stretched, headed for the door. "I think we're up against crazies like we never saw before. I think they'll have some more surprises for us."

With a quick salute, he said good-night. As he walked to his own motel room, he was deep in thought. Organization, discipline, patience. Sometimes they weren't enough. The Able Team needed some luck, and fast.

3

Fists slammed at the door. In one motion, Lyons rolled from the bed, grabbing his .357 Magnum as he fell to the carpet. A passkey rattled against the door's lock. Two young FBI agents in gray three-piece suits rushed in. One of them pulled the drapes open, letting in the brilliant morning sun. The other kicked the bed, shouted: "Up, Lyons! This is an emergency! Sorry to have to. . . ."

The agent saw the bed was empty, then started, backed up as he saw the Magnum pointed at his face.

"You don't know how sorry!" Lyons put the pistol on the bedtable as he reached for his pants, his trim blond hair still rumpled from sleep. "You wake people up like that, someone just might put you to sleep. Ever hear of a wake-up call? Maybe just knocking on the door?"

"Good morning, Mr. Lyons," Anders said pleasantly. Anders motioned to the two agents to leave. "The helicopter's waiting for you. For you and your team."

"What?"

"Commander Brognola called. He tells me he is shifting your team to the New York area. The helicopter will take you to an airfield. A jet will take you directly to New York City."

"Are Rosario and Gadgets ready to go?"

"Mr. Blancanales and Mr. Schwarz, I believe, are already at the helicopter."

"What happened with that freighter?"

"It was burning out of control when the Coast Guard reached it. We were unable to board the ship before it sank."

Minutes later, Lyons sprinted from his motel room and ran across the beach. The helicopter sat at the water's edge, its rotor spinning. Blancanales and Gadgets climbed in as Lyons ran up. Gadgets extended a hand to him, and Lyons pulled the side door closed as the helicopter lifted away.

Lyons leaned close to them, shouting over the noise of the rotors. "What's the word?"

"They didn't tell me anything," Gadgets replied.

"Told me to move it," Blancanales said. "Forget breakfast, forget my suitcase, just move it."

"Something must be going on up there." Lyons strapped himself into his seat, took his cordless electric razor out of his coat pocket. "Wonder what?"

Barracks and equipment yards flashed beneath them. Soon they were over the asphalt airstrip of the Army base. A small Air Force jet pivoted at the end of the strip, then taxied into take-off position.

The helicopter dropped down fast, the copilot throwing open the side door even as the skids touched the ground.

"Okay, hotshots!" the copilot shouted. "That's your plane."

The Able Team double-timed it to the jet. It was Hal Brognola himself who let down the plane's folding steps. There were no greetings, only:

"In there. Take a seat. There's an information folder for each of you."

Lyons waited while Brognola retracted the steps and secured the outside door. "What's happening in New York City?" he said.

Brognola was grim. "Bad news."

The three Los Angeles hardmen followed Brognola forward. Four chairs were arranged around a conference table. Brognola spoke quickly into an intercom, then went to the door leading to the pilots' cabin. He locked it.

"Anders tell you what happened last night?" Lyons asked.

"He briefed me," Brognola took his seat, opened his folder. "The first page in your folders is a map of the Wall Street area. The World Financial Corporation Tower is circled in red."

Engines shrieking, the jet accelerated down the strip. Brognola didn't pause, only spoke louder. "At ten o'clock this morning, a van parked in the underground garage of the Tower. The company security guards checked the identification of the crew, allowed them to proceed with their unloading. The guards saw four movers.

"One guard accompanied the crew into the building. The guard who remained in the garage saw the crew take several large shipping crates in. The crates were labeled as business machines and appeared to be very heavy. Each crate was lifted with the truck's hydraulic lift and a dolly.

"Before the other guard returned, a telephone crew arrived, supposedly to service the building's internal telephone lines. There were three persons in

the crew, one man, two women. All had correct identification.

"It was not until the seven people were inside the
building that the guard realized they were all Latins.
Perhaps of Puerto Rican nationality. The guard
called the Tower's Director of Security, told him
about them. During his conversation, all the telephone lines went dead. The guard could not call the
police. So he attempted to leave the garage. One of
the telephone crew pursued him.

"The supposed telephone service person attacked
the guard with a knife, wounding him. But the man
ran from the garage and summoned police.

"The first police unit to arrive was driven back by
automatic weapons fire. Police have sealed the building and the immediate area."

Brognola paused. He glanced to the others, closed
the folder. "We have reason to believe these seven
persons to be the terrorists responsible for the series
of bombings in New York City.

"We checked with the World Financial Corporation, and they say there were about thirty employees
in the building—including the building security
guards, computer service personnel, and executives
doing weekend work. We must now consider all
those people hostages."

"Hal, you said bad news." Lyons flipped through
the pages of information in his folder. "This is good
news. We've been running all over the East Coast trying to track these crazies down, and now we know exactly where they are. At least, we know where seven
of them are. Gadgets, what do you think you can do
about all this?"

"Well...." Schwarz gave it a moment's thought, then grinned. "I can bug the telephones, wire the place for sound, monitor the entire electro-magnetic spectrum, and maybe even take their pictures if they get close enough to the windows. I can do that as soon as I get there. But if you want some *fancy* tricks, let me look the situation over and give it some thought."

"That's the stuff!" Blancanales laughed, his genial Latin face creasing in appreciation.

"About the phones!" Gadgets jumped out of his chair. "They cut the phones from the inside, right? As long as the phones are out, they can't call out. So *we* cut them, of course—make sure the phones stay dead—and you know what? They have to use a radio."

"That's already accomplished," Brognola told him.

"All right!" Gadgets raved. "And I'll ECM them so tight—you see what I mean? They're trapped in there. Lotsa problems: if their main man is outside, they'll have to get instructions...."

"I'll have equipment for your electronic counter-measures when you get there, Schwarz," Brognola nodded. "The reason we cut the phone lines to the building is *secrecy*. This is important for you three to understand. The situation has been sealed, the Tower and the immediate area isolated. Federal officers have replaced all Police Department personnel. Reporters, so far, know nothing of the building's seizure or of the hostages; and to prevent citywide panic, that is how it's going to stay. The executive officers of WorldFiCor have pledged their cooperation, naturally. And as the financial district is deserted for the weekend, there is no reason why the secrecy should be broken. Do you understand?''

''You mean, no matter what we do, no one is to know?'' Lyons asked. ''I like that.''

''The only way to go,'' Gadgets added.

''Except,'' Brognola pointed out, ''we cannot maintain secrecy after dawn Monday. That gives you—'' he glanced at his watch ''—say, forty-one, forty-two hours.''

4

Dropping into a canyon of stone and glass highrise towers, the shuttle helicopter's rotor blast created a storm of litter and filth around the waiting limousine. Lyons didn't wait for the skids to touch asphalt, but jumped the last five feet, ran to the limo. The slightly heavier, more easy-going Blancanales followed a few steps behind. And Schwarz, distracted as always by his mental machinations, took up the rear, fast.

A young man in a chauffeur's uniform hurried from the front seat to open the door for them. Lyons jerked it open and got in.

"Where's the information?" Lyons demanded.

"On the seat, sir. That folder—" the young man pointed "—is WorldFiCor executives, worldwide holdings. The other folder is all Puerto Rican nationals and other persons known to sympathize with or participate in FALN operations in the United States...."

"Go to the helicopter," Lyons interrupted. "Help that man with the cases."

"Yes, sir!" The agent ran to the helicopter, helped Brognola unload two aluminum cases, then hurried back to the limo, a case in each hand. Hal Brognola, burly in his business suit, followed him to the car carrying his own briefcase.

"Get this car moving!" Lyons shouted through the rear of the helicopter lifting away.

"That's Mr. Smith," Brognola told them, nodding at the agent behind the wheel. The limo accelerated even as Brognola pulled the door shut. "You will not use your names around him or any of the other agents helping you."

"Pleasure working with you, Mr. Smith," Blancanales smiled.

Smith answered without turning his eyes from the avenue. "I'm not working with anyone. I'm on vacation in Hawaii."

"You will use the following names," Brognola continued, pointing first to Lyons, then to Blancanales, then to Gadgets. "Hardman One, Hardman Two, Hardman Three. Mr. Smith will be Hardman One's personal liaison to the back-up services."

"Great," said Lyons in the clipped manner of the tough big-city cop he would always be. "But we need another car, right now." He turned to Blancanales. "You got what you need? You ready to go to work?"

Blancanales looked up from the folder of photos and typed biographies. "Sure, soon as we get there," he said suavely, unruffled by the pace of his hardman life.

"We're here," Smith announced. He put a handset to his mouth. "Car number two please."

A yellow cab swung away from a line of unmarked cars, screeched to a stop only steps from the limo door. Agents in an assortment of uniforms, suits, and bums' rags opened the opposite door, took Gadgets' aluminum cases.

Gadgets flashed his usual nervous grin as he left. "Airborne!"

Blancanales gave Lyons a quick salute, then Lyons was alone in the back seat.

"How's that for service, sir?" Smith asked.

"A little slow. Take me to the President of World-FiCor, now."

"Moving, sir." Smith power-drifted through a sweeping U-turn, using all four lanes of the avenue. "Would you like me to drive past the Tower? Take a look at it?"

"I don't have time to play tourist," said the blond mission leader.

Thirty-five floors above street level, a casually dressed Schwarz, carrying his shabby satchel of gadgetry, looked out at the black glass and steel of the neighboring World Financial Corporation Tower. He and Brognola stood in the commandeered office of an investment broker directly across from the Tower. Agents had already shoved aside the desks and cabinets. Boxes of electronic gear, plastic-wrapped consoles and coiled cables crowded the office.

"You have a view of the front entrances," Brognola told him, pointing down to the base of the Tower. "The entire face of the building, and something of the top."

"I need a map, a big map. And. . . ."

"Right here." Brognola unrolled a hand-drawn chart of the area.

"And who is my liaison man?"

"Mr. Jones!" Brognola shouted. Instantly a young agent, in a janitor's gray coveralls, ran into the office.

"Yes, sir!"

"What's going on with the roof-top antennas?" Gadgets asked. "When will we be operational?"

"We're bringing the cables down right now."

"And the micro-waver interlock with the antennas on the other buildings?"

"Functioning."

Gadgets grinned. "Okay! Get those cables down here!" He ripped the plastic sheeting from a console, uncoiled the power cord, and sought out the wall plug.

Bumper to bumper between a produce truck and another yellow cab, Blancanales and his agent waited for the light to change. On both sides of the street, neighborhood people—Puerto Ricans, Cubans, Central American Latins, Mexicans—filled the midday sidewalks. He saw Spanish signs, Latin grocery stores, full-figured women shopping with their plastic mesh bags. It could have been any street in Latin America. But they were less than five minutes by subway from the WorldFiCor Tower.

"So, what's your name?" Blancanales asked his driver.

"Mr. Taxi, sir."

Blancanales laughed. "Appropriate! You speak Spanish?"

"Sí."

"Do you have a weapon?"

Mr. Taxi slapped his jacket. "Sidearm, sir. Uzis in the trunk. Five hundred rounds, each weapon. Tear gas, too. We're loaded for bear."

"How about some telephone change? I need to make some calls."

"No need, sir." The driver took a briefcase from the front seat, passed it back to Blancanales.

It was a mobile phone. "Convenient, but is it secure?"

"Scrambler interlock. NSA equipment. If it ain't safe, nothing is." Blancanales opened the folder and called his first contact.

A butler ushered Lyons into the walnut-paneled library of E. M. Davis, President of the World Financial Corporation. Davis, an elegant man with thinning, sandy hair, left his armchair and crossed the library.

"I'm very pleased to meet you, Mr. Stone," he said to Lyons, shaking his hand.

"It is unfortunate that I have to speak with you, sir."

"That is the world we live in." Davis sighed, then turned to the other two executives in the room. "Mr. Robbins, Vice-President, Western Hemisphere. Mr. Utek, Data Systems. I believe the three of us can answer all your questions concerning this problem. Please take a seat, Mr. Stone. What can we tell you?"

Lyons glanced around the room. There were high French windows overlooking the manicured rose garden and rolling lawns of the Long Island estate. One wall held floor-to-ceiling shelves of leather-bound law volumes. Mementos, photos and degrees covered another wall. One photo in a gold frame showed Davis standing with his arms over the shoulders of a past President and Secretary of State of the United States. All three men wore party hats and grinned into the camera. The ex-President held up two fingers behind Davis' head, like rabbit ears.

Tucked away in the lower left-hand corner of a mass of photographs was one wood-framed black-and-white that seemed conspicuous to the sharp-eyed Lyons by virtue of its very privateness. It showed a rather younger, much less bald Davis with a pretty young Latin woman and a young teenage boy; the boy had the dark skin of the woman but, remarkably, Davis' light, sandy hair. It was the only photo in the collection of this particular group. Lyons stored the image of it in his mind, along with the inevitable impression created by the picture of Davis with a former U.S. President.

"First," Lyons began, "why do you think these terrorists chose your company as a target?"

Robbins glanced at Davis; Davis nodded. Then Robbins answered: "We do have investments in Puerto Rico. Until today we believed we followed a socially progressive policy toward the Commonwealth and the people of Puerto Rico. We have never questioned the politics of our employees or associates. We have never attempted to influence the regional politics. We instructed any corporate officer, if questioned, publicly or privately, to state simply that the World Financial Corporation supports the right of the people of Puerto Rico to determine their future by the ballot box. We do business with—and within—most of the nations of the earth. We are sure we can continue in operation in Puerto Rico, whether it is the fifty-first state or an independent nation. We thought this was a fair position."

"Terrorists don't care what's fair," Lyons told him. "Perhaps that's exactly why they hit your company. Have Puerto Rican groups ever made any demands or threats against your company?"

Davis answered. "Nothing, Mr. Stone, that our internal security services did not neutralize."

"What do you mean?"

"We are in the business of international finance and management. We operate on a vast, worldwide scale. In some ventures, we are partners with nations. If WorldFiCor were to be granted nationhood, our company's income on operations and investments would exceed the tax revenues of most nations.

"Early in our company's history, I realized what an attractive target we would be. Though we do not have tanks and jet fighters, we have a security service superior to those of most nations. However, that service operates in our foreign branches. We had hoped that, in New York, the United States Armed Forces would protect us from military assault. I can assure you, whatever the outcome of this crime, it shall not occur again."

"Terrorists can strike anywhere," commented Lyons.

"Our foreign offices have never had this problem. We have not allowed it."

"I understand. Now the guards, your company guards who were on duty at the time—they have told us the terrorists unloaded several large shipping crates. We have to assume these crates contain in excess of a thousand pounds of explosives. Though I don't think they can destroy the entire Tower, they could—"

"A thousand pounds of dynamite!" Utek, Vice-President of Data Systems, turned white. "No one told me!"

"C-4," Lyons corrected him. "It's a military explosive, more explosive in fact than dynamite. That much C-4 could do serious, possibly terminal damage to the Tower. It is certainly enough to kill every person in there. We'll need complete—and secret—cooperation from some of your company's personnel."

"I'll tell you what the threat is!" Utek stood, pointed at Lyons. "I'll tell you. It is complete and utter chaos! Those maniacs could ruin us! You cannot comprehend what this means...."

"I can comprehend what will happen to those people if that C-4 goes off. We wouldn't find enough of them to fill a sandwich bag."

"What do they want?" Utek demanded, glaring at Lyons. "How much? We'll pay. A million? Ten million? It's petty cash compared to what it'll cost the company to reconstruct the data for this fiscal year alone."

"They don't want money! That's the problem. We're dealing with *terrorists*. They won't negotiate, they won't talk, they...."

Davis quieted both Utek and Lyons with an upheld hand. "Gentlemen! Of course we're concerned about our personnel. But, Mr. Stone, I don't believe you truly do understand the nature of this threat to our operations.

"Our Tower is not merely an office building. It is a data center. It operates twenty-four hours a day. It generates its own power. It is meant to be safe from earthquake, or natural disaster. It has to be. That Tower, and our system of satellite communication, serves two thousand worldwide offices. Any transaction anywhere on this globe is relayed, recorded and analyzed instantaneously.

"If anything happens to the Tower, we are, quite simply, out of business. And that would create very serious repercussions in the economy, in employment, in the morale of the multinational business community. It would take years to recover. This is a very serious threat to the economic security of the United States and its allies."

Lyons looked at his watch. Thirty-nine hours, twenty-one minutes to go. "I need access to your personnel records, if that's possible. I need the blueprints of the Tower. If the architect and general contractor are available, that's great. The heads of building maintenance and security, too. And it all has to be secret. Total cooperation and no questions."

"Of course, Mr. Stone." Davis walked Lyons to the door, opened it for him. They entered the mansion's central hallway. Persian carpets covered the polished marble floors. The butler walked a few steps ahead of Davis and Lyons.

"Within this hour," Davis said, "we'll have the blueprints for you. The personnel records will be more difficult. We'll need to have that information transmitted from Kansas. Our long-term data storage banks are in the salt caverns there. And that information will be no more recent than twelve months ago, the end of the last fiscal year. The fiscal year runs July first to June thirtieth rather than January first to December—"

"I know."

"Of course. I simply don't want any confusion. We will also prepare a map of the floors and areas devoted solely to data services, and instructions for those officers forced to enter those areas, so that they will not inadvertently endanger the survival of the data systems. We will also have an emergency crew standing by in case of damage to the systems. You must understand what a disaster this could be to our corporation, and to the capitalist enterprise in this country. Is there anything I've forgotten?"

The butler opened the ten-foot-high hand-carved entry doors. Lyons squinted against the afternoon light.

"Yeah. How about the names of the people that the terrorists have trapped in the building? Can't forget about *their* survival, can we?"

5

This is how it happened, hours earlier.

On the fifty-third floor of the Tower, Charlie Green, Director of Eastern European Accounts for the World Financial Corporation, watched a video display screen. *Saturday morning—what a time to be watching blocks of numbers and commodity codes rolling upwards on a screen and listening to a Russian clerk calling long-distance from Hungary!* The Russian spoke English with a heavy French accent.

"Mr. Green, this is a State problem. It does not concern your company. If you will be patient. . . ."

"One hundred and fifty thousand United States dollars this joker carries off in his briefcase, and it doesn't concern us? Please explain that, comrade!"

"I assure you, the security forces of the People's Socialist Republic of Hungary will not allow the money to leave the country."

"Where is the money? We're not talking about bankruptcy, but I want to know about the cash. He had the money in the briefcase, and police have him. Do they have the money?"

"The matter will be investigated completely, I assure you. The dollars United States will be returned to your company. It is very important for the State to clear this problem."

"If you want to do business with WorldFiCor again, your government *will* clear this problem. Do we understand each other?"

"You have my complete understanding."

Green hung up, left his desk. He wore gray sweatpants, a bright red sweatshirt. His running shoes felt clammy on his sockless feet. His suit hung in his office closet. More than twelve hours before, the Vice-President of European Operations had told him they had a problem with an account in Hungary. Would Mr. Green check on it before he left for the weekend?

"Sure, I'll check on it. I'll chase the jerk to Siberia, is what I'll do," he said to the air.

"Did you call me, Mr. Green?" Mrs. Forde, his senior office assistant, came into the office. Mrs. Forde, a forty-year-old mother of two, trim and athletic in her tailored gray skirt and jacket, held stacks of printouts. In the outer office, automatic typewriters printed information from Hungary as it simultaneously appeared on the video display.

"The commies are driving me blinkers," Green said.

"How can I help?"

"You can't," he told her, and tried to put his hands in his pockets. There were no pockets on his sweatpants. "Yes you can. Is there a delicatessen where I can get breakfast? How about you? Have you had a chance to eat this morning?"

"No, thank you, sir, I'm skipping."

"You? Why, are you dieting?" Green glanced at her. She had a figure like a twenty-year-old. Maybe better.

"Oh, no, sir," she smiled. "Last night, it was dinner, a concert, disco dancing, then a party with *so* much to eat. Would you like for me to send one of the temporary girls?''

"No. I'll be back in half an hour.''

As he walked through the outer office, the temporary girls glanced at his mismatched sweatclothes, flashed him polite smiles. But they didn't pause in their work, stacking and collating sheets of information on the embezzlement and bankruptcy in Hungary. He stopped in midstride.

"Anyone want coffee? Food, anything. I'll treat.''

One of the temporary girls, a dark-haired twenty-year-old in thick glasses, struggled with two heavy boxes of printouts. "I'll go for you, sir. Just give me a list. I'm going down to Xerox anyway.''

Green took one box from her. It weighed at least thirty pounds, solid paper. "Negative. I'll fetch my own breakfast. I'll carry this down for you.''

"Oh, thank you!''

"Oh, damn!'' Mrs. Forde exclaimed. "What's wrong with the phones? Jill! When you're at Xeroxing, call for service on our phone lines.''

"Yes, ma'am.''

Green opened the office door for her. They went to the elevators, a straight bank of six on a single wall, one of the elevators for executives only. Green passed his magnetically encoded ID through the Executive elevator's sensor.

"Stand by for a thrill,'' Green joked. "The exec car drops fast.''

"Thank you for helping me, sir. It's very considerate of you.''

"Your name's Jill?''

"Yes, sir."

"You know what's going on?" Green asked as they got in the elevator. "Xerox is fifth floor, right? All this weekend work is happening because some Hungarian Communist Party official—who happened to be a banker, you figure the ideology on that one—he decided to skip the People's Paradise. Problem is, with all the high-tech communications this corporation's got, it's all numbers. Numbers in, numbers out. Doesn't mean anything if someone's putting in make-believe numbers. Personally I think it's more than just this Hungarian..." he added cryptically.

The elevator dropped. For a second, they almost floated from their feet. Jill laughed.

"An executive toy," Green joked. The elevator slowed as it came to the fifth floor. "Are you a temporary from outside the company, or a temporary from the secretarial...?"

Green turned as the elevator doors slid open, saw the woman in the telephone company uniform. "The telephone company is already here."

He saw it as if in slow motion: the Latin woman in the uniform turning, the .45 rising as she took a combat crouch.

Green hit her with the box of papers. He shoved the box straight out from his chest, thirty panic-thrown pounds of paper striking the .45 even as the slug left the muzzle of the pistol.

Paper exploded. Sheets and shreds of printout flying, Jill screaming in the elevator, Green jumped on the woman in the phone company uniform. He jerked her head back with one hand, then he had her pistol in the other.

He pointed the .45 at the Latin woman's head. "What the hell! Who are you?"

His peripheral vision saved him. Even as he stood, he saw a second Latin in a phone company uniform. Green snapped a shot at the man, threw himself backwards into the elevator, screaming at Jill: "Hit the button! Hit it! Up! Get us out of here!"

Slugs punched into the elevator doors as they slid closed. The single bullet Green had fired missed the man, continued twenty feet down the corridor and struck a nylon bag. The slug smashed several electronic components in the bag.

Julio knew the next hour would be the most critical. They had hoped to avoid discovery until after the placement of the C-4 and thermite charges. But hopes do not win liberty. Nor do hopes guarantee the success of a military operation. Their leaders had anticipated all possible problems and police reactions. They had trained Julio and his squad to succeed despite accident and opposition.

When the garage guard alerted the police, Julio and Luisa kept the first police cars at bay with their automatic rifle fire. Julio then hurriedly placed claymore mines in the garage and basement entrances, and retreated to the lobby. Julio and Luisa took positions in the chrome and black-marble lobby. All pretense was past. Julio still wore his mover's coveralls, Luisa her phone company uniform. But they now wore .45 automatics, carried M-16 rifles.

Julio watched the elevators. There were six pairs of elevator doors on one of the Tower's twin cores. There were six pairs plus the wide doors of a freight elevator on the wall of the other core. Both sets faced each other across the marbled corridor between.

Luisa moved throughout the lobby, scanning the plaza surrounding the Tower for police units. "They made it so easy for us," she said to him as she passed. She motioned to the high walls of glass. Only the two elevator cores isolated in the center of the lobby blocked the view of the plaza.

Julio had no time to reply. He was watching the elevators' indicator lights. In one elevator, his comrades rode up, distributing loads of C-4, thermite, and detonators. But other lights also moved through the series of plastic numbers. One car left the thirty-first floor, stopped at the twenty-eighth floor. Then it moved again. A second car left the eighty-fifth floor, came down without a stop.

Julio checked his tape roller. His leaders had anticipated all situations and had included a tape roller in Julio's equipment; it was used by freight packagers to seal boxes quickly.

Silently arriving in the lobby, the first elevator's doors opened. Julio pointed his M-16 at the chest of a secretary. She was alone in the car.

"Don't move!" he said. "Come out of the elevator! Here!" She obeyed, too surprised even to speak. He slammed the tape roller down on her shoulder and walked around her, holding the roller in one hand, his M-16 in the other. Before she realized what he was doing, her arms were taped tightly to her body with nylon reinforced freighting tape. Then her hands to her body. He turned her, put a loose loop of tape around her legs. She could hobble, but not run, not even walk fast.

"Oh, please! No! I don't have anything. I don't...." Julio slapped a patch of tape over the secretary's mouth.

He saw other lights appear on the elevator indicator, one starting at the fifty-third floor, dropping fast. He kicked the secretary's feet out from under her, let her fall to the marble floor.

"You try to move, you die!"

He crossed to the door of one of the elevators that was coming down, but it stopped at the fifth floor. Then, suddenly, the doors of another car opened. Loud voices broke the lobby's silence.

Two executives, immaculate in their conservative gray suits, left the elevator arguing. Julio ran to them, shoved them.

"Watch where you're going, spic punk!" one of them swore. Then the executive saw the M-16, staggered backwards, dropping his briefcase.

Julio jammed the long gun barrel into the man's chest, jarring him backwards into the black marble wall. The man sank to the floor, his hands out in front as if to shield himself from the automatic rifle.

The other executive sprinted away, his overweight body lurching with every stride.

"Harvey! Don't run!" the executive on the floor screamed.

Intestines and excrement sprayed from the running man's body as Julio fired a six-round burst through his gut. A second burst from Luisa's rifle threw the carcass sideways across the polished floor. Bullets exiting from the victim ricocheted off the tall, tinted, shatterproof windows on two sides of the lobby.

"Nooooooo!" The surviving executive half-screamed, half-sobbed. Julio went to him, kicked him hard in the solar plexus. He fell sideways, his body heaving as he tried to vomit and breathe at the same time. Julio wrapped him up with tape, shoving him from side to side.

Julio's hand-radio buzzed. The voice of their squad lieutenant whispered through the earphone. "This is Zuniga, on the fifth floor. One of them has escaped. He took Ana's pistol. You must kill him. . . ."

But the light blinked from the number five, flashed into the higher numbers, into the upper ninety-five floors of the Tower.

Ana, on the fifth floor, shoved an extra thirty-round magazine into her phone company uniform. She jerked back the cocking lever on her M-16, and punched an elevator's "up" button. She waited.

"Back to your duty!" Zuniga ordered.

"I'll kill him! I'm going up to find the. . . ."

"No! You had your chance to kill him, and he took your weapon. Now return to your duties. Nothing else is important."

Her face remained hard, livid with anger. Zuniga coaxed her. "We'll hit the alarms soon. That'll bring them all out."

"And if he hides up there?"

"Then he's blown to bits."

Ana smiled, flipped back the safety on her M-16. She returned to her task of distributing one-kilogram blocks of C-4 around the two columns of elevators.

The detonators were Zuniga's responsibility. He returned to the unit he had been assembling. It was then that he saw the torn nylon bag.

He ripped open the Velcro flap. The radio-trigger fell to pieces in his hands.

The loss of this one single component threatened their entire mission. Zuniga forced himself to remain calm. It would be impossible for their leader to smuggle another detonator past the police lines which surely surrounded the Tower already. He thought of executing Ana, or forcing her to remain behind and trigger the blast. But no, she had not been careless. The man had surprised her while she worked.

He considered alternatives to radio detonation. He had been well-trained. He knew of a hundred ways to trigger the C-4. But it must be a technique or device which would both insure the success of the mission *and* his own survival.

Zuniga's laughter rang in the silent corridor. He threw down the shattered component. He intended to execute all the hostages anyway. He would use their *fear* as the detonator.

"We have terrorists downstairs!" Quickly Green related to his overtime office staff what had happened on the fifth floor. "I saw two. There could be any number of them in the Tower—five, ten, twenty crazies. And they have automatic rifles."

"There's no money in the building!" Sandy interrupted. She was a tall, slender blonde, one of the temporary workers who rotated through the various offices of the Tower. There was panic in her voice.

"There's nothing here they could want. . . what could they possibly want?"

"We'll hear all about it on television tonight," Green told her. "WorldFiCor is an international corporation. What they want could have nothing to do with us. All that we have to do right now is live through it."

"But they know we're here," Jill said. "They know what floor we're on! From the elevator numbers!"

"I hit all the numbers when we got out," Green told her. "The elevator stopped on every floor above us."

"If we hide," Sandy interrupted again, "the police will be here soon. They've got to be!"

"Sandy, let me finish. We don't have to be brave, but we have to keep cool. We have to think out what we'll do. We can stay up here, or we can try to get out. If we stay up here," Green detailed his thinking, "we might be here for days. They might have time to search all the offices. But if we try to get out, we're betting our lives that the crazies won't be waiting for us. We'd have to shoot our way past them, and I've only got six rounds in this pistol."

"Seventeen bullets," Mrs. Forde corrected. She took a snub-nosed .38 revolver from her purse. "Five in the cylinder, and six extras. And I know how to use it."

"Mrs. Forde!" Green said in mock horror. "Pistols are illegal in New York City."

"Yeah. Murder and rape, too. And what about terrorism?"

"We still don't have fire superiority," Green continued. "But if they find us, or we have to break out, we could surprise one or two of them. Surprise them to death. So what's it going to be? It's time for a vote."

"No voting!" Mrs. Forde told him. "You're the Department Director. None of the girls has got your experience. We'll do what you say."

"This is not an accounting project. And it's their lives we're talking about, Mrs. Forde."

The woman turned to the others. "Mr. Green was a company commander in the Army. Two tours of duty in Vietnam. If you don't want to do what he says, take the elevator downstairs. Maybe you'll make it to the street, maybe you won't."

Diane, the third temporary worker, smiled, gave Green a quick salute.

"You got my vote."

Sandy and Jill raised their hands.

Green nodded. "Command accepted, with reluctance. And now, troops, get comfortable. Your fearless leader has to think of what to...."

Screaming drowned out his voice. It was an electronic wail. In every office and corridor of the hundred floors, sirens sounded the alert to evacuate the Tower.

"Fire! They've set fire to the—" Jill shrieked, running to the door.

"Shut up!" Green shouted. He grabbed her, pushed her back into a chair. "Really, Jill, keep cool! It's just noise, a fire alarm. It could be a trick. When we smell smoke, then we'll panic."

Green knew that the building was considered fireproof. Something else must be up.

One by one, in twos, sometimes in joking and laughing groups WorldFiCor employees and executives left
the elevators. Every one of them assumed the evacuation of the Tower was a weekend drill. Within seconds of stepping into the lobby, each employee
became a prisoner. The soldiers of Zuniga's squad
seized and immobilized the employees with freighting
tape. They did not resist. It happened too quickly.

Zuniga waited for a proper subject for his upcoming demonstration. His improvised plan required
horror. It was not enough that the prisoners saw the
corpse of the fat executive sprawled on the lobby's
polished marble floor. They might think the fat man
provoked his captors. The prisoners might hope for
mercy. Without blind, unthinking terror twisting
their emotions, torturing their intelligence and logic,
the prisoners might not take the desperate chances his
plan demanded.

A woman screamed. Zuniga watched his soldiers
throw a young black woman against the wall. She
was very young, perhaps still in her teens. They
silenced her screaming with a rifle butt to the
stomach, then a loop of tape around her head to
cover her mouth. Loops of tape immobilized her
hands.

Cocking his .45 automatic, Zuniga started toward
her. But to his side, elevator doors slid open. An
elderly woman stepped out. She walked slowly, her
back stooped from decades of bending over a desk.
Under one arm, she carried an account folder, sheets
of paper and adding machine tape hanging from the
folder. Two of his soldiers, Carlos and Rico, grabbed
her, wrenching her arms behind her.

She cried out in pain, and Carlos released his grip. The old book-keeper fell to her hands and knees. Rico jerked her to her feet. Screaming, anger and horror on her face, she tried to twist away.

Zuniga glanced at the prisoners. All of them watched Rico struggling with the old woman.

Crossing to her in three strides, Zuniga jammed the barrel of the .45 automatic into the old woman's mouth and blew her head away.

6

Returning to downtown Manhattan, Lyons called Gadgets on his limo's secure phone.

"Hardman One for Hardman Three, connect please!"

"This is Mr. Three's liaison, will you hold for a moment?"

"Get me the man, right now!" Lyons glanced at his watch. Thirty-nine hours, two minutes. He looked outside. Double-parked trucks and jaywalkers jammed the traffic. Whenever Smith saw an opening, he accelerated, whipping the limousine through the traffic like a sports car. But then a traffic signal or a shopper's open car door or kids on bicycles slowed them again.

Gadgets finally came on the phone. "This is Hardman Three. How's it going?"

"Slow. I had a conference with the executives of the Corporation. That is one company I wouldn't want to work for. What's happening there?"

"Nothing electronic. Two or three words on handradios since I got plugged in. They've got an iron fix on it in there. They also got a body count going."

"Don't tell me the details over this line. Wait until. . . ."

"This line is secure. I checked it out. National

Security Agency equipment. Unless someone has one of the three phone units, all they can tap in on is static."

"Go on then."

"I hear we got two bodies in the lobby. A man and a woman. It happened before we arrived."

Lyons felt his gut twist. Two working people dead. Dead because they cared enough for their company and their duties to put in a sixth day this week. Not that their company cared about them. Dead because of political problems thousands of miles away. Dead because a group of psychopaths wanted to dictate the future of millions of Puerto Ricans.

And how many more innocent people would die?

"You there?" queried Gadgets.

"I'm here. Those psychopaths make any demands yet?"

"No communications whatsoever. We got a negotiation team waiting."

"Buzz me if anything else happens. I'm going to join up with Hardman Two. Off."

Lyons adjusted his shoulder holster, checked his pockets for speedloaders. Only four. Six rounds in his .357, twenty-four rounds in the speedloaders. He called forward to Smith:

"Got any .357 Magnums? Or .38 rounds?"

"9mm only, sir."

"Call the taxi. Fine out where Hardman Two is, tell him I'm on my way. Then trade in this tank for something less conspicuous. Pick up a box of .357 ammunition."

It took Smith thirty seconds to get Blancanales' location. Lyons noted the address and cross street.

"Drop me off at the corner, I'll take a real taxi. Get back with the other car within half an hour."

"And that's fifty rounds you wanted, sir? .357 Magnum? Sounds like you're worried about some serious trouble."

"I'm not worried about anything. I'm going to *make* some trouble."

In the glass of a shop door, a shirtsleeved Blancanales spotted the two young men following him. He glanced into traffic, saw his driver park the phony cab on the other side of the street. The two young Puerto Ricans stayed a hundred yards back. They walked from block to block with him, stopping from time to time at a shop or market, blending with the pedestrians and young layabouts on the street.

Blancanales came to the tenement where Bernardo Commacho's mother lived. This was his third stop in Spanish Harlem. He knew Commacho would not be there. Though Blancanales had a list of names and updated addresses of known FALN couriers and soldiers, he expected to find none of them. He expected them to find him. And they had.

Children playing in the tenement's rooms covered the sound of his steps. He went up the stairs slowly, checking the stairwell for the most likely ambush site. Perhaps they would try to take him on the way down.

When he knocked, the apartment's door opened only a few inches. The door chain allowed it to open four inches.

"*Buenas tardes*, Señora Commacho. *Puedo hablar con su hijo,* Bernardo?"

"All my children are gone, moved away, long time ago."

Beyond Mrs. Commacho's gray hair, he saw a shelf crowded with photos of her sons and daughters. One photo, framed in black, shared an alcove with the Madonna and Child. Candles burned for that dead son. Blancanales had read about the boy in his information packet; only sixteen, he died when he assaulted a police squad car with a .22-caliber rifle modified to fire full automatic. He wounded one officer, then the rifle jammed. Both officers had emptied their service revolvers into him.

"I'm not with the police, *señora*."

"Then why do you ask about Bernardo? Only the police care where he is."

"I talked to his friends, only a few minutes ago. They told me your son visited you last week. If he's still in New York, I want to talk with him. It's very important."

"Who is it important to?"

"To Puerto Rico."

"My son was born in this country. He knows nothing of Puerto Rico."

"Perhaps you could call him. Then we could talk."

"He never calls. He never visits. . . . It is very difficult for an old woman when her children are so far away."

"Well, maybe I will see you again, Mrs. Commacho."

After the door's bolt locked, he waited. No voices. He heard her steps across the floor. A chair squeaked when she sat down. No other footsteps.

On his way back to the stairwell, he took a newspaper from a doorway, rolled it tight. He started down the stairs.

He smelled the cologne of the young men. He maintained his pace down the stairs, making his steps loud in the stairwell. There were no shadows, no places for concealment there. When he came to the second-floor landing, he passed the hallway fire door, took three more loud steps, then spun around.

Even as the Puerto Rican kid jerked open the fire door and rushed onto the landing, Blancanales brought the rolled newspaper down on the boy's revolver. The pistol hit the floor. The kid gasped as Blancanales rammed his knee into his crotch. Then stepping behind the boy, the hardman locked an arm around his throat, lifting him from his feet.

An instant later, a second boy tried to sprint up the stairs. Blancanales flung the first boy at him. They both tumbled down the stairs. Before they hit the next landing, Blancanales followed them, kicking one, then the other as they rolled. He jumped on them, slipped plastic handcuffs on them.

Stunned, the first boy lay still. The second attempted to twist from the plastic around his wrists. He couldn't. But his legs thrashed out at Blancanales as he tried to stand. Blancanales kicked the boy in the nose, breaking it. Blood poured from his face.

Someone moved behind Blancanales. Spinning, he dropped to the stairs as he pulled his Browning double-action and aimed.

Hands in his slacks' pockets, Lyons leaned against the wall, grinning. "An excellent demonstration! How to capture two suspects without getting your hands dirty.... However, you died while you were playing football with that punk's head. The third man came up behind you and shot you all full of holes."

"There isn't any third man," Blancanales told Lyons as he stood up, returned his Browning to his shoulder holster. He dusted off his sports coat. "And these two aren't suspects. I don't suspect them of anything. I *know* they are FALN. Give me a hand, we've got to drag them down to the cab."

Blancanales jerked the belt from the pants of one of the youths, cinched the boy's feet to the banister. Then he and Lyons pulled the other kid to his feet, walked him down the stairs.

"Not the cab," Lyons told him. "They've got a Cadillac parked at the curb. Back door's unlocked. We'll stack them up in the back seat."

At the tenement's entry, a third youth lay on his face, unconscious. His hands were tied with his shirt. Blancanales saw the boy, started, then grinned almost foolishly at Lyons.

"Ignore that punk," Lyons said with a straight face. "You said he doesn't exist."

They followed the yellow cab to a street near the docks. The agent in the cabbie's uniform parked, then started back to the Cadillac. Lyons motioned him away, left the Cadillac. Blancanales stayed with the three FALN soldiers.

"Can't have those three getting a look at you," Lyons told the agent.

"Yes, sir. Of course. So here it is." The agent glanced towards the steel door of a warehouse. "I called ahead and they sent out a man to unlock it. You won't be disturbed in there. The previous tenants imported very illegal substances—they won't be back for ten to fifteen years. I'll be parked right here in case you need the secure phone. Anything else you need, I don't want to know about it.''

"What do you mean by that?'' Lyons demanded. The agent started away. Lyons grabbed his arm, jerked him around to face Lyons again.

"You do what you have to do in there,'' the agent told him. "But it's not on my conscience. I volunteered for this case. But I didn't volunteer for what you're doing.''

"You think we're a death squad? You think we're going to take those three boys in there and torture them?''

"Why did you ask for this place? That's exactly what I think.''

"Let's hope that's what they think, too.''

Lyons went to the steel door, dragged it open. Blancanales drove the Cadillac in. Lyons secured the door, walked through the warehouse's dim, reeking interior, checking the side doors. All chained and padlocked.

In the office, he found the tools and electronic devices he had requested. There were pliers, tin snips, hammers, and a butane hand torch. Also several coils of wire. For a moment, Lyons marveled at Gadget's micro-electronic wizardry, then he took wire and pliers and returned to the prisoners.

Blancanales dragged the three young men out of the Cadillac. He dropped them on the concrete. Lyons looped baling wire around their wrists and ankles.

Their wallets told them the youths' names. Bernardo, whom Blancanales had choked and thrown down the stairs. Manuel, whose face was now a mask of clotted blood from his broken nose. And Carlos, barely conscious, who bled from a long, shallow cut on the side of his head.

Lyons paced around the three boys, his hands in his pockets. He grinned like a devil. "Now boys, we talk. What did you want with my friend?"

Blancanales sat on the Cadillac's hood, watching the three boys.

"We tell you nothing!" Bernardo shouted. "Do what you want with us!"

"That's right, Bernardo." Lyons laughed. "We'll do what we want. And it will be you first."

They dragged Bernardo to the warehouse office, shut the door behind them. Blancanales wired the youth to a chair while Lyons fitted together the components of the butane torch.

"I'm ready to die for Puerto Rico," Bernardo declared.

Lyons turned on the torch, lit it. He twisted the knob until the flame became a tiny blue point.

Bernardo watched Lyons and the flame, the young man's eyes looking from the tall hardman to the point of intense blue fire hissing from the nozzle of the torch. Bernardo drew a shuddering breath, closed his eyes. He forced his breathing to calm. But he began to shake, as if from extreme cold, first his thighs, then his jaw. He tensed his shivering legs, clamped his jaw.

Lyons waved the flame past the young man's shoulder, the acetate of his shirt shrivelling. Bernardo flinched, his eyes opened wide for an instant. He closed his eyes again, ground his teeth.

"Wait." Blancanales pushed the torch away.

"What?"

"Perhaps we can reason with the boy."

"Forget it. Don't have time."

"Just wait." Blancanales turned back to the youth. "Who sent you out to take me?"

Bernardo didn't answer.

"Why did they send you to take me? Wouldn't it have been easier to shoot me? You could have shot me. *But they told you to take me alive. Why?*"

"I do as my leaders tell me."

"You're a good soldier, you do as you're told. Now you're in real trouble, you know that?"

"Keep your talk! I'm no fool! I will tell you nothing! Burn me, kill me! I am only one soldier, millions fight for Puerto Rico. *Viva Puerto Rico libre!*"

"Enough of this talk," Lyons interrupted, playing the heavy. "It's time to get this barbecue in motion."

"No!" Blancanales pushed Lyons back. "Boy, this is the truth. I want to talk to your commander. You take me to him, and you live. Your friends live."

"I will not betray...."

"No one's asking you to betray...."

"None of this!" Lyons stepped between Blancanales and the youth. "No deals! We'll get the information out of him. We'll cook him alive. He'll talk!"

Blancanales shoved Lyons aside. "You and me, kid, we go to your commander. Look at me, you can trust me. No betrayal. You blindfold me, lock me in a trunk, whatever is necessary to protect your commander. Your friends stay here. When I come back, your friends go free. No jail, no prison, no torture.''

"And what if my commander tells me to kill you?'' Bernardo asked.

Lyons laughed, sneered at Blancanales. "What do you say to that, nice guy?''

Taking the young man's possessions from his pocket, Blancanales found Bernardo's wallet and opened it. Inside there were photos of the boy's family, girl friends. Blancanales held up a photo of Bernardo standing with his mother, father, younger sisters and brothers.

"If I don't come back—'' he pointed to Lyons, ''—first he kills your friends, then he kills your family.''

Lyons grinned, wickedly.

Bernardo looked from Blancanales to Lyons, then back. "Can I talk with Manuel and Carlos?''

Blancanales snipped the wires binding Bernardo to the chair, then the wires around his ankles. "Go talk with your friends. We'll wait here.''

From the office, they watched Bernardo squat beside his friends on the floor, talking with them. Lyons twisted the butane valve, watched the flame shrink to nothing.

"Acting like that gives me the creeps,'' he whispered to Blancanales. "Next time, you're the sadist.''

"But you're so Aryan, such a monster!'' Rosario joked. "I thought you'd actually fry the kid if I didn't work something out. But a softhearted old Latin like me. . . he knows too well!''

Lyons looked at his watch. Thirty-eight hours, twenty minutes. He glanced out at Bernardo. "If he won't take you to meet his commander, then we have to get the man's name from him. Whatever it takes. Whatever has to happen.''

In the silence of the warehouse, the three boys' Spanish echoed. Finally, Bernardo returned to them. He nodded.

They went to the steel door, shoved it open. As Bernardo followed Blancanales out, Lyons stopped him. He put his fist against the boy's chest.

''My friend comes back. You understand? Do you understand me?''

''*Entiendo.*''

He snipped the wire from the boy's wrists. Lyons waited until they walked around the corner, then sprinted to the waiting taxi, abandoning the securely tied Manuel and Carlos.

''You saw them?''

''Following!'' The cabbie whipped a turn, accelerated.

''No need to stay close, I've got D.F.'s and mini-mikes on my partner. And give me the phone.''

Lyons dialed for Gadgets, got him on the first ring. ''Hardman Two's out and running. The boy said he'll take him to his commander.''

''How's the signal?'' Gadgets asked.

''Checking.'' Lyons held the phone hand-set under his chin, pulled the directional finder out of his pocket, flicked the switch. A steady beep-beep-beep-beep sounded for a moment, then fell off, the intervals between pulses becoming longer.

''Up ahead,'' the cabbie called back to Lyons. ''They just took off in a taxi. How much distance do you want me to hold?''

"Keep them in sight, but keep traffic between you and them. If they make a turn and we miss it, we can pick them up with the D.F."

"What about the minimikes?" Gadgets asked.

"Just a second! I'm doing three things at once." Lyons switched on the receiver. Faint voices in English and Spanish came from the speaker. "Can hardly hear it. How close do we need to be?"

"Depends. How much concrete between them and you, how much other electronic activity. Play it by ear, as they say."

"Are you free? Can you get in a mobile unit?"

"You think you need me right now?"

"Hey, Hardman Two's going right into the mouth of the beast. He needs all the back-up he can get."

"On my way!"

Lyons broke the connection and dialed Agent Smith, his driver and liaison man. "Where are you? What kind of car you got now?"

"At the intersection of Broadway and Fourth. I'm driving a red ten-year-old Dodge. I'm wearing white painter's coveralls."

"Be ready to move. You got my box of magnums?"

"Yes, sir. What's going on? Sounds like things are getting hot."

"Hot? My partner's walking into hell. And we're going in two steps behind him."

7

Turning every few seconds to scan the traffic behind them, Bernardo gave the cab driver directions that weaved through the financial district. At one corner, the NYPD's phony power company barriers were up. The WorldFiCor was only a block away.

Blancanales looked past the barricade, saw a utility vehicle. There were no workers in the truck. Further up the street, two men in utility workmen's uniforms leaned against a parked car. Two men in suits sat in the front seat of the car. Blancanales looked over at Bernardo, watched him. But Bernardo only glanced at the barricade and told the driver to make another turn.

Several blocks later, they stopped for a traffic light at the edge of Chinatown. The cab driver turned to Bernardo and asked him, "Boy, do you know where you're going? Is someone following you? Are you looking for someone? What's going on with you?"

"It does not concern you," Bernardo snapped. "You're a driver, drive!"

"Sure, kid. Anywhere you want."

"Stop!" Bernardo shouted. "We get out here." He gave the driver a 10-dollar bill, and they walked through traffic to the sidewalk.

Bernardo scanned the cars and trucks passing

them, then led Blancanales across the intersection. Again, he watched the traffic passing them, looking at several cars, staring at the faces of the drivers and passengers. He turned from the street, looking at the shoppers and tourists and neighborhood kids on the sidewalks.

Across the street, Blancanales saw Lyons pass in the phony yellow cab. He glanced at Bernardo, winked to Lyons. Lyons raised his eyebrows slightly as he hid his face behind a newspaper.

"Where now?" Blancanales asked Bernardo.

"Wait here." Bernardo went into a corner luncheonette and moved to the phone. He dialed a number, watching Blancanales while he talked.

Blancanales leaned against a light pole, talked to himself. The minimike was in his inside coat pocket.

"He's making a call. I tell you, this kid is one very paranoid young man. But he doesn't know anything about counter-surveillance. I think he's just a street kid that they recruited. Also, when we went past the WorldFiCor, he didn't even notice."

Looking back to the luncheonette, he saw Bernardo hang up and step outside. "Talk to you later, he's coming back."

Bernardo returned and held up a hand for a taxi. "The meeting is set," he told Blancanales. "But first, we...."

"We must lose any surveillance?"

"My commander instructed me to be very careful."

They took a taxi to the next block, got out, ran through traffic to the entry of a tenement. Bernardo led him through the central hallway to a back stairway. Up the stairs to the second floor, through a window to a fire escape, down the fire escape to an alley. They crossed the alley.

Bernardo pulled open the unlocked rear door of a restaurant and hurried through the kitchen. The cooks and dishwashers turned their backs. Blancanales saw a waiter go to the rear door, lock it. Then they wove between the tables. The few patrons didn't look up from their lunches and conversations.

Out on the street, Bernardo flagged another taxi. "Where to, kid?"

"Drive." Bernardo pointed straight ahead.

"We're sight-seeing," Blancanales explained.

"Tourists, huh?" The driver commented. "Where you from?"

"My friend here's from New York," Blancanales said, "but I'm from California."

"California! First time in the big city?"

"No. But it's the first time I've had time to look around. Any tourist attractions around here?"

"Hey, man! This is Little Italy. Unless you're into crime, you know, gangsters, the mob, Mafia, you got to go uptown for tourist action."

"This is Little Italy? This where Lucky Luciano grew up?"

"Out!" Bernardo interrupted. "We're getting out here."

They dodged traffic as they crossed the avenue. Bernardo led Blancanales around a corner, and without breaking stride, pushed him through the side door of a waiting florist's van. Bernardo slid the door closed, then got into the driver's seat. They were alone in the van.

There were no windows in the back of the van. As Bernardo started the engine, he leaned back and said tersely, "If you try to look outside, no meeting. If you try to signal anyone, no meeting. Understand?"

"Entiendo."

Bernardo jerked a curtain shut, then raced into traffic. Blancanales rode in the dark van, his companion a funeral wreath.

Cruising through the narrow streets of shops and tenements, Lyons watched the sidewalks and cars for his partner. The afternoon's heat had thinned the pedestrians. Kids sat on steps sipping Cokes. Teenagers gulped from bag-wrapped beer cans, passed wine bottles. But he saw no Latin ex-Green Beret in a business suit walking with a twenty-year-old FALN soldier. He glanced into the cars in traffic, trying to keep his face concealed behind the headlines of that afternoon's paper. He knew the boy would be watching the traffic for surveillance: for him to see Lyons might mean death for Blancanales. Lyons knew his threats had impressed Bernardo, but the boy was only one of the soldiers in this operation. The others might not give a damn about Bernardo's friends and family.

The D.F. signal faded.

"Go north a few blocks," Lyons told his driver. The secure phone buzzed. Lyons grabbed it.

"This is Hardman Three," Gadgets said.

"Where are you?"

"Driving north on Broadway. Where are you?"

Lyons glanced out at a street sign. "We're going north on Allen. The D.F. signal's picking up. Must be gaining on it. Do you have a D.F. receiver you can pass to Smith?''

"Sure do. I'll call him, arrange a pass. You have anything on the minimike?''

"Nothing. You ready for action?''

"I'm ready for anything. Things are popping all over. You got the news yet?''

"What now?''

"They made some demands. Finally. The Bureau has a negotiation team talking with them now.''

"Give me the details in person. Keep moving, let's try to keep the D.F. between us.''

Lyons broke the connection, punched the code for the phone with Mr. Smith in Little Italy. "You still parked, Mr. Smith?''

"Yes, sir. Waiting for instructions.''

"We're driving north on Allen Street. Make some speed, come up behind us. I'm in the yellow cab. When you get here, Hardman Three has a D.F. receiver for you. Further instructions when you make it up here. Hit it!''

The D.F. beeps came faster and faster, became a buzz. Lyons pointed to the curb. "Pull over! We must be within a hundred feet of them.''

Even as the driver swerved, the signal slowed. Looking back, Lyons saw traffic stop at a red light. The D.F. signal held a steady beep-beep-beep-beep. The lines of traffic at the light included a meat truck, an old Plymouth stationwagon, and a florist's van, in addition to the many passenger cars.

"Make a U-turn!'' Lyons shouted.

"You want me to call for Bureau backup? We could use some more cars.''

"No!" Lyons punched Gadgets' code on the secure phone. "We reversed direction. We're coming up behind some trucks. Signal very strong." Then he punched Smith's code. "Smith, *Smith*! Park. Wait for us to pass."

"Parking now. You got our man in sight?"

"Maybe. Watch for us."

The phone buzzed. "Hardman Three here. I'm on the Bowery, that's a block or two west of you. I'm continuing south."

"Get Smith's cross street," Lyons told Gadgets. "He's parked. Try to get there and give him that D.F. receiver. I think we're bumper-to-bumper with them."

The traffic light changed to green. Weaving the cab past slower vehicles, the driver brought them up behind the meat truck. Lyons stayed low in the seat. The D.F. signal shrieked.

"Stay behind this truck," Lyons glanced out the window, but he could not see the florist's van or the old stationwagon. "Just keep it on the truck's bumper until something changes. Any chance you got a periscope in the trunk?"

"No, sir. But I'll call for one...."

"That was a joke!" Lyons exclaimed, wide-eyed. "You Bureau guys crack me up. What happens when you can't get exactly what you need, right away?"

The cabbie-agent laughed. "Never happens. If we don't have it, we make a call. Like you guys. We called you."

Lyons smiled coolly, slid lower in the taxi's back seat as the Plymouth came up on their left. A white-haired black man was driving. Newspapers and cardboard filled the back of the car. Through the taxi's open window, Lyons heard Chinese phrases coming from the stationwagon. The old man repeated each Chinese phrase. Lyons glanced over, saw the old man look at a three-by-five flash card, then say a Chinese phrase.

"I don't think that old man's with the FALN," Lyons told his driver. "Pull ahead of him, there's a flower-shop truck up there."

"What about this truck?" The cabbie indicated the meat truck.

"Keep it in the rearview mirror, we'll maybe follow it if it makes a turn."

His driver whipped the taxi past the stationwagon. Ahead of them, the florist's van raced through the intersection to beat a yellow light. The shriek of the D.F. signal modulated, became a fading beep-beep-beep as the truck sped away.

"That's the van!" Lyons grabbed the secure phone.

"Want me to run the light?" the cabbie asked.

"Stay back. I'm calling the others." In a second, he had Gadgets. "You've got a white and green florist's truck coming down on you. I didn't see the driver. There's no windows in the back of it. It's the truck we want."

"I see it!" Gadgets shouted, then the line cut off.

Suddenly Lyons' phone buzzed. "This is Smith. Your partner—he just pulled a screaming U-turn through four lanes of traffic. What's going on? What do you want me to do?"

"He gave you a D.F. receiver?"

"Yes, sir. I had a signal, but it's fading."

"Stay where you are. I think Hardman Two is going to be doing some circles."

"What if he takes one of the bridges into Brooklyn?"

"If he does, Hardman Three is on him. You stay where you are." Lyons leaned forward to his driver. "Drive over toward East Side Drive. That'll put us right under the bridges, right?"

"On my way."

The D.F. signal became a distant beeping. Lyons buzzed Gadgets. "Where are you? You staying behind them?"

"It's the truck, no doubt about it," Gadgets told him. "He's pulling turns and stops, trying to spot us."

"Is he heading toward either of the bridges?"

"Nope. Not yet. We just circled a block. Hey, he's going back up Allen. He's going north on Allen. Can you take him? He might have spotted my car."

"Smith's still on Allen, where you left him. You fall back. What kind of car do you have?"

"A Volkswagen beetle—with a Porsche engine and transmission. These feds have all the toys."

"Don't get a speeding ticket. Off." Lyons keyed Smith's code. "Smith! They're coming your way, get ready to move. You got the description? A green and white florist's truck, no windows in back."

"Yes, sir! Behind him already. Keeping a half-block distance behind him. He turned east, he's on Delancy. He could be headed for the Williamsburg Bridge. I'm on Delancy. He's turned again. South now."

"Don't turn. We'll be there in a minute. Stay near

the bridge, he might be doing a last loop or two before going over the river."

"Parked and waiting, sir. Signal's holding steady."

The phone buzzed when Lyons broke the connection. "Hardman Three here. I think the signal's holding steady. I mean, I'm moving east, but I don't think *it* is moving at all."

"He was on Delancy. He turned south." Lyons glanced at his pocket street map of Manhattan. "Get out to Grand, and head west. I'll be one street north, criss-crossing. Off."

Smith buzzed him. "He passed me! But there's no signal from the van. Do I follow?"

"Get behind him! Stay with him until we can figure this out."

"Moving!"

Lyons turned up the volume on the minimike. The faint traffic and truck sounds were gone. Now, nothing. He listened, the speaker pressed to his ear.

Clang! The metallic sound made him almost drop it. He held the minimike's receiver away from him, turned down the volume. He heard what sounded like steel on concrete. Footsteps. Then more sounds of steel. The sounds faded to almost nothing. Lyons buzzed Gadgets.

"You monitoring the minimikes?"

"Too faint for me. You get something?"

"I think the boy dropped him someplace, then took off. He passed Smith, on Delancy, but he had no signal. Nothing. Smith followed him over the Williamsburg Bridge. I don't know where they are now."

"Let's pull some circles around that block. On my way up."

"Head toward the Williamsburg Bridge," Lyons told his driver. "You have some equipment with you in this cab?"

"Yes, sir. Two Uzis, ammunition. Four Army-issue tear gas grenades. Two walkie-talkies. First aid kit. If there's anything else that you need...."

"I know, you can call." Lyons punched the code for Smith. "Where are you now?"

"He's taking me for a scenic tour of Brooklyn. He turns once in a while. Nothing serious. I'm staying a block back."

"Here's what I want you to do. Call one of your feds. With a civilian car, civilian clothes. New York identification. Have the fed crash into the truck. A fender bender. I don't want that boy driving around anymore. I want him out of the game. Maybe he has an outstanding warrant on him, could you arrange that?"

"Yes, sir. No problem."

"Then do it. Off."

They drove through a neighborhood of old tenements and garages. Lyons monitored both the D.F. receiver and the minimike. Faint, very faint noises came from the minimike. But the D.F. beeps came strong.

"Circle this block," he told the cabbie-agent. The D.F. signal wavered, then came back strong as they completed the circle.

"Sounds like he's in one of those buildings," the cabbie commented.

Lyons scanned the doorways and windows of the

tenements. One city block, all the buildings four or five stories high, each tenement floor having four to ten apartments: there were hundreds of rooms to search.

"Yeah, but where?"

In the sealed back of the van, Blancanales had lost all sense of direction and distance as the boy wove through the streets of the city. But he knew the D.F. unit and minimike would help his partners follow him; as long as he had those micro-electronic units, he was not alone.

The van skidded through a high-speed right turn, swerved wide, then whipped right again. The speed threw Blancanales against the side of the van. His hands mashed flowers as he braced himself for the next turn. But the van accelerated, hit a driveway ramp at more than forty miles an hour and went airborne. Blancanales hit the roof of the van, then the floor, hard.

Skidding threw him forward. He hit the back of the driver's seat. Before he could right himself, the side door slammed open. Two men wearing black ski masks grabbed him, pulled him from the van.

He went from the dark interior of the van to the dark interior of a garage. A third man in a ski mask threw the van door closed, then dragged down a heavy steel door as the van screeched away. The exchange took less than ten seconds.

One holding each arm, the ski-masked FALN soldiers hurried Blancanales through the dark garage reeking of oil and gasoline. He could see cars and trucks with the hoods up. The third FALN soldier ran past them and leaned into a car.

Headlights blinded Blancanales. He felt hands pat him down, slip into his pockets. Hands took his Browning double-action, then his wallet, his keys, pocket change. They found the minimike, took it.

Handcuffs locked his wrists together. The soldiers searched him again. They jerked his suitcoat back and down. Ripping open his shirt, they slid their hands over his dark-skinned chest, both shoulders, his back.

They found the D.F. antenna. Pinned to his shirt collar, the hair-fine wire ran down his body to the plastic-cased transmitter clipped to the elastic of his underwear. They tore the antenna and D.F. unit from him.

One of the FALN soldiers motioned, and the light died: Blancanales felt a hood slip over his head.

8

Whipping in behind the yellow cab, Gadgets ran from his supercharged Volkswagen and jumped into the cab's back seat. He carried his khaki canvas satchel. But Lyons wasn't in the taxi.

"Where's my partner?" Gadgets asked the cabbie-agent.

"Which one?"

"Hardman One."

"He went in." The cabbie-agent glanced to the block of tenements.

"*What!*"

"He took a hand-radio, checked his pistol, told me to wait here, told me to tell you that things had changed. Here's the other radio, if you want to quiz him."

"I got one." Gadgets pulled a hand-radio from his satchel, but didn't key it. He checked the other units first. He clicked on his D.F. and minimike receivers. The D.F. signal gave a steady beeping. The minimike receiver was silent.

"Hmmmmm." Gadgets took another unit from his bag. He twisted a dial, waited. Silence.

"Problems?" Taximan asked.

Gadgets held up the unit. "This is a super mini-mike receiver. If that minimike was still on our man, we would be getting a heartbeat. But if we aren't...."

"Trouble, huh?"

"Well, if he's in bad trouble, it's too late to help. But more likely they gave him a skin search. Stripped him and checked him for electronics. Those people aren't dumb. However, they're not as sharp as Able Team."

The hand-radio buzzed. "Taxi! Hardman Three there yet?"

"I'm here. Where are you?"

"Watching two friends watch you. You bring anything interesting with you?"

"All kinds of tricks."

"Sit tight for a minute. Give the hand-radio to the cab driver. I'm pulling a one-man ambush, and I might need some help...."

Lyons whispered the instructions to the cabbie-agent, then waited. A hundred feet across the tarred tin roof of the tenement, two Latins leaned over the edge, watching the street five floors below. One of the men spoke into a walkie-talkie.

That was Lyons' signal. He crawled from his cover behind a crumbling roll of roofing paper. Thirty feet away, near a fan housing, there was an ice chest that the men must have parked there. A few cola cans lay around it. He crossed the thirty feet and took cover behind the fan housing. He crouched, waiting, his .357 in his hand.

Slow, even footsteps crossed the roof. Lyons heard someone remove the ice chest lid, pop the top of a can. Then the man came into view as he went to the edge of the roof. He glanced down into the alley. He jerked back, called out, "Juan! The taxi!"

The other man ran across the roof, and he too looked down. Lyons waited until both men's backs were to him; then he made his move. He came up behind the first man and smashed him in the head with the magnum. The man fell limp, landing on his back.

As the neighboring man turned, Lyons threw a low round-house kick into his knees, grabbed him by the collar, and crushed his nose in with his elbow. Lyons threw the man down on top of the first.

Lyons looped plastic handcuffs around the wrists of the top man, threw him to the side. The other man twisted, suddenly pushing Lyons back. As the man reached to his waist for a pistol, Lyons pinned him with a knee, leaning all his weight on the man's arm, and simultaneously hammering him on the top of the head with the four-inch barrel of his magnum.

Stunned, the man went slack long enough for Lyons to flip him over, slip plastic handcuffs around his wrists and jerk the plastic loop tight.

Searching them quickly, he found two .38 pistols, a sheath knife, a walkie-talkie. Neither man carried identification. Lyons looked over the edge of the roof; within seconds he saw the taxi cruising through the alley. He buzzed them on his hand-radio.

"Hardman Three up, please."

One of his prisoners, blood streaming from his nose, struggled to his feet and tried to run. Lyons kicked his feet out from under him, put a foot on the back of the man's neck, pressed his face into the tar roof. Lyons took two plastic handcuffs from his pocket, then dropped down on the struggling man's legs and looped his ankles together.

The other man was not yet conscious. He bled from several cuts under his hair where Lyons had pistol-whipped him. Lyons cuffed that man's ankles together also. Then he returned to the conscious prisoner.

He flipped him over and put the six-inch blade of the sheath knife against the man's throat:

"Where are the others?" Lyons shouted at him.

The prisoner put his head back and yelled: "*Viva Puerto Rico libre.*"

"What're you *talking* about? All day long I've been meeting Puerto Ricans who are trying to die for Puerto Rico. What's the point of a free Puerto Rico if you're dead?"

The man spat at him. Behind Lyons, someone clapped. He spun, pointing the knife. Gadgets stood there grinning, his satchel hanging from one shoulder.

"Do you want to continue your political discussion, or can we get to work?"

"Yeah, yeah. These jerks. So—you get anything?"

Gadgets nodded, took a few steps away from the prisoners, motioned for Lyons to come over.

"Sure did. The D.F. is across the alley there, somewhere on the first floor. I got a narrow-beam scanner that works like a flashlight—except in reverse, see."

"Don't tell me about it. Let's get going. You think you can get any information out of these two?"

Gadgets shook his head. He slipped a unit out of the canvas bag and went over to the edge of the roof. He pointed it down to the alley, moving it slowly from side to side. The unit beeped. Gadgets sighted down the unit like a pistol, then turned to Lyons and called him over.

"There, right there." Gadgets pointed. "Looks like thirty or forty feet from that steel door, straight into the building. That's where the D.F. is. But that doesn't necessarily mean anything."

Gadgets glanced to the walkie-talkie Lyons had taken from the FALN sentries. He grinned, told Lyons:

"I got a plan."

Lyons went down the stairs two at a time, the bulging pockets of his light suit coat knocking against his hips with every step. After Gadgets had detailed his plan, Lyons took both of the captured .38 pistols, extra plastic handcuffs, the sheath knife, and his hand-radio. If he could get into the building across the alley before the FALN soldiers inside checked with the sentries he had just immobilized, then he had a chance of taking them by surprise over there. But he had to move fast. The extra fifteen pounds in his pockets didn't help.

He walked swiftly through the lobby, alert for FALN soldiers. They could be anywhere. On the street he hurried through the late-afternoon strollers and shoppers. Anyone around him could be a sentry. Any of them might have a pistol and instructions to shoot, then warn the group. If they spotted Lyons as a law officer, he had no defense. He wouldn't see the bullet coming.

Around the corner, he glanced into the alley. The steel door was the third entry from him. He continued along the avenue. The third business from the corner was an auto repair shop.

The first business was a café. Above the café were apartments. No one at the lunch counter looked at him as he passed. The next business was a wholesale auto parts distributor. The door was closed, the windows barred.

At the auto repair shop, he glanced at the steel roll-away door. Padlocked.

He saw wet tire tracks crossing the driveway. The tracks started at the trickle of filthy water in the gutter, continued to the steel door. The car had driven from the street, into the garage. Lyons glanced to the street's asphalt. There were no streaks from wet tires leaving the driveway.

Above the garage, the windows on the second and third floors were bricked in. But the fourth and fifth floors had windows. One window had an iron railing interwoven with flowering vines. A fire escape zigzagged down the face of the building. The lowest rung of the steel ladder was more than ten feet above Lyons.

He noted all this in three seconds as he walked past. Then he backed up and stared at the fire escape.

The ladder hung only three and a half or four feet above his reach. He climbed onto the iron security grill of a shop's back window and reached up for the ladder. He couldn't quite make it. He braced himself, jumped for it.

He missed the grip, fell hard to the asphalt. Getting up before he could feel the hurt, he grabbed the iron grill again, swung up one foot.

A pistol jammed against his head. He hung there,

both hands on the ironwork, one foot on the window's brick edging, waiting for the bullet to crash through his skull. There were footsteps behind him.

"Don't resist, officer," a quiet, melodic voice cautioned him. "Step down from the window. You're coming with us."

The slender, white-haired Ramón and Rosario Blancanales were walking in the direction of the distant WorldFiCor Tower.

"I'm Ramón. I'm very glad you came to speak with us." He was looking at Blancanales with a calm strength. "Have no fear. If we wanted to kill you, we would have done so already. We sent the young men to bring you to us because we want to help you."

"How can you help me?"

"We can help each other," Ramón corrected. He seemed oblivious of his personal bodyguards patrolling about them as they walked. "You have those terrorists in the World Financial Corporation Tower...."

"What do you want? What are your demands?"

"We have no demands."

"Then why are your people in there?"

"But they are not our people."

Blancanales stopped and stared at this man Ramón.

"They are not our people," the Puerto Rican repeated. "It is not our operation. And what they are doing is not for the good of Puerto Rico. The FALN knows of the bombings that were not announced in the news. For the past few weeks we have tried to find these people who claim to be members of our organization. We failed. And we know from our sources that the police and the feds have failed to find them also. We cannot allow them to continue. We have decided to offer you all the information that *Las Fuerzas Armadas de Liberación Nacional* has. We represent all the people of Puerto Rican blood who seek liberty for their nation. Though we—our organization and our soldiers—are your enemy, we do not believe that the actions of this group claiming to represent Puerto Rico will help our struggle. We have limited our military actions to targets that are facilities of the United States Armed Forces or represent the repressive forces of the Federal government.''

''Not cafeterias and tourist buses?''

''We believed at first that those incidents were actions by the secret police to discredit our organization.''

''What secret police? You mean the FBI?''

''Not the FBI. *You.* You are not in the FBI. You are not the police. Yet you receive the complete cooperation of the police and feds. Perhaps you will tell me what government service you represent?''

''No.''

Ramón laughed. ''Then please do not object when I refer to you as secret police.''

''Call me anything you want. I call you terrorists. Now, what information do you have?''

''This.'' Ramón reached under his coat, took out a nine-by-twelve envelope, and gave it to Blancanales.

They were at the end of the alley. A taxi waiting at the curb rolled forward. Ramón pulled the door open, spoke quickly to the driver in Spanish, then turned to Blancanales. "This driver will take you back to where we left your weapon and possessions. In the envelope, there are instructions on how to contact us if you need us. Remember this, Mr. Secret Policeman. We are everywhere. Though today we help you, perhaps tomorrow we kill you. Especially considering your brutal treatment of Bernardo, Manuel, Carlos. You should take very great care. *Adios*."

When Ramón slammed the cab's door closed, Blancanales ripped open the envelope, skimmed over the pages and photographs. There were photos of 11 Latins, men and women. Their ages varied from 17 to 34 years old. All had joined the FALN volunteering to serve as soldiers. All of them, when assigned to surveillance, courier work, research, or the neighborhood cádres had, according to these typed reports, either refused to serve or shown no enthusiasm. Many of the 11 had protested to their officers that they had volunteered for weapon and explosive training, and had no interest in the routine work of a political organization.

At the end of all the recruits' probationary periods, their officers had clearly recommended against advancement or weapons training. The officers decided the recruits were possibly federal agents or psychopaths, stamped their files "Unreliable."

Anthony Zuniga:　32, born in New York City, Vietnam veteran, trained in explosives, dishonorable discharge, one year in stockade while investigated for torture and murder of Viet Cong prisoners (evidence included severed body parts, snapshots of castrated prisoners). Served eight years in prison for armed robbery and mayhem. FALN sources discovered that Zuniga had worked as assassin for right-wing Cuban exiles. Has displayed charisma in attracting and influencing others.

Julio Torres: 19, born in New York, junior high-school dropout, bragged of "making his first kill" at 13, no history of employment other than robbery and drug sales. Illiterate in English and Spanish.

Luisa Diaz: 20, born in Los Angeles, high-school dropout, graduate of California Youth Authority, served four years for armed robbery, murder, and participation in gang rapes (gang paid her to lure victims into the gang's trap). Heavy PCP user. Threatened FALN officer with physical violence when he told her there was no place for drugs in a revolutionary organization.

Felipe Parra: 21, high-school dropout, discharged from U.S. Army for striking an officer. Bragged of killing police officer in an ambush. Arrested for possession of sawed-off shotgun, jumped bail. Criticized organization, said: "If I could steal an atomic bomb, I'd give the gringos a choice between keeping Puerto Rico or losing New York."

Fernando Tur: 19, arsonist. Joked that his favorite sport was soaking derelicts with gasoline and burning them alive.

Ana Commacho: 23, five years in Youth Authority for murder of father when she was 13. One year in prison for ice-pick robbery of elderly. Bragged that she "never got caught again, because now I kill them."

Carlos Calazda: 30, Vietnam veteran. Dishonorable discharge. Trained as sniper, infiltrator. Investigated for atrocities; but investigating Staff Sergeant and Lieutenant died in an anti-personnel grenade explosion while visiting Da Nang restaurant: three other U.S. personnel killed in incident: friend of Calazda suspected of throwing grenade (Mario Silva).

Mario Silva: 31, Vietnam veteran. Trained in demolitions, indicted for murder of several U.S. personnel in Da Nang. Dishonorable discharge. Served two years for auto theft and rape. While in prison, attempted to join Mafia.

Rico Zavala: 19, five years in Youth Authority for torture of teenage girl. After release, went to armed robbery and murder. Clipped photos of victims from newspapers. Repeatedly asked FALN superiors to send him to assassinate U.S. government officials. Said to FALN officer: "If we kill all the Yankee bosses, then we can be the bosses."

Pedro Ortiz: 22, record of armed robbery. Fascinated by rifles. Self-trained sniper. Subject to fits of depression and rage. Respects only violence.

José Herva: 34, long-time FALN operative. Trained in organization and mission planning. Became compulsive gambler. Suspected of skimming contributions to FALN.

Of the 11, only José Herva had served with the FALN for any significant length of time. The others, denied advancement after their probationary periods, had been expected to drift away after their officers cut them off from pay, training, and meetings.

However, the 10, and José Herva as well, had apparently all disappeared at the same time.

The engrossing report he was reading, as he sat hunched in the back seat of the cab, distressed Blancanales for reasons not entirely to do with this mission. As counselor and volunteer organizer for a Catholic youth group back in his native Los Angeles, this man of action was known even to the kids as the Politician because of his ability to intervene in the lives of youths who were going bad. But there were some sad failures he seemed powerless to prevent, and this inventory of youthful corruption within the ranks of the FALN reminded him of it. He knew only too well that violent behavior would always, finally, meet with its violent fate. And this never ceased to cause him regret.

Now Blancanales understood why the FALN would help the Able Team: psychopaths murdering diners and elderly tourists did not produce good propaganda for them.

In a few minutes, the taxi made a turn into a narrow alley and stopped at the open door of a garage. Blancanales left the taxi without a word. He went into the garage.

He found his pistol, wallet, and the D.F. and mini-mike on the hood of a car. But before he could return his possessions to his pockets, he heard someone running in the alley. He spun, leveling his Browning at the entrance.

"What's going on here?" Gadgets ran into the garage. His canvas bag was wrapped around an Uzi, concealing it from witnesses.

"Now, nothing." Blancanales holstered his pistol.

"I had my conference, they brought me back. And do I have information!"

"Yeah? Well, they got Lyons."

"Shot him?"

"I don't know. But something's gone wrong. We thought you were in here. Twenty minutes ago we took out the sentries, then Lyons came down and was going to get in quiet, bring you back. And suddenly, no Lyons!"

They returned to the alley. Gadgets tried the hand-radio again, pressing the transmit button several times, shouting into the unit, "Hey! Where are you? Come in!"

No response.

"When he checked in, he told me he was still on the street."

"Those guys in there—the Puerto Ricans—they didn't take him. You won't believe it, but they're on our side. I'll explain later. Where's our backup?"

"On the other side of the block. Come on, we've got to backtrack him."

Gadgets jogged away, clutching the canvas bag around the Uzi. He glanced at the doorways and fire escapes. Blancanales slipped the envelope into the waist of his jeans and followed his partner. He left his pistol in its shoulder holster: whatever was going to happen to Lyons had already happened.

Several fire escapes were suspended on the sides of the alley. Blancanales scanned the landings. On the higher floors of the buildings, he saw laundry, potted plants, furniture. He heard television voices and the rhythms of Latin music. But there was no one at their windows, no one standing in the back doorways.

Ahead of him, Gadgets spoke into his hand-radio, then went around the corner onto the avenue. Blancanales poked along, looking into doorways, glancing into trashcans. He saw something odd.

A textbook lay on the filthy steps of a basement's freight entrance. It was new, the pages stiff, unmarked by underlining or notes. Blancanales examined the area closely.

On the brick edge of a window, there were footmarks in the accumulated soot and dirt. At the top of the window's security bars, someone's hands had left two smeared spots in the filth coating the bars. There was a fire escape directly above the window. On the lowest rung of the steel ladder, there was a smear as if someone had clutched it.

And then he saw something else: on the bricks of the tenement, on the sheet steel of the basement door, and on the asphalt of the alley, splattered drops of blood.

9

Lyons breathed. He felt air moving through his mouth and throat. He strained to fill his lungs, but there was an immense weight on his chest. Trying to move his arms, he felt steel cut his wrists. Handcuffs. He wondered why they had bothered. For they had shot him in the back of the head.

How long until he died? Seconds? A minute or two? How long until his life drained through the hole in his skull?

He had no vision. Only thoughts. Thoughts of life in this last second of living, telescoped by onrushing death to trick him into thinking he had minutes left.

Sensations came to him. He heard quick sing-song conversation, not English. Chinese? Japanese?

A low, unheard vibration. A lurch forward, then a stop. He was in a car or truck. He could smell the exhaust. The vibration came from the engine idling.

The weight on his chest shifted. Someone was kneeling on his chest, to immobilize him. Perhaps he was dying, perhaps not. Then it all came back to him.

In the alley, he had felt the pistol against his head, had stepped down from the barred window. When they grabbed his arms, he twisted away from the pistol, slammed one man's face with his elbow, saw blood. Turning, he kicked another man, chopped an arm holding a pistol. He saw an Oriental face and grabbed it by the hair, and in the instant that he jerked the head down into his upcoming knee, Lyons had felt the back of his head explode. Then he had fallen into the void.

They had captured him. They put him in a car. They wanted him for interrogation. He had seen enough eye-gouged, blow-torched, pliers-mangled corpses in his years to know what might soon happen to him. If he fought now, in this car, his struggling might only bring the coup de grace, the second bullet. But that way he would escape the long hours of horror.

Thrashing suddenly, he heaved the man off his chest, then twisted on the seat and kicked out. He felt his feet smash glass. He kicked again and again, wildly. He connected with someone's head, someone else's arms. Another man grabbed Lyons by his hair, hit him.

But the fist glanced off his head. He could see! The glancing punch had half torn off a rag covering his eyes. He could see an arm swinging a pistol. He twisted again, blocked it with his shoulder, kicked out again.

Hands closed around his throat. He heaved and thrashed but couldn't break the grip. He had only seconds of consciousness left.

Lyons had not served a decade with the Los Angeles Police Department without learning that handcuffs could be broken. He'd seen crazies do it. Was he strong enough? Was he crazy enough? Despite the thumbs crushing his throat, he relaxed his shoulders, forced his handcuffed wrists down over his buttocks. He strained down with the muscles of his back and torso, while pulling up with his arms and shoulders. The pain became a white light.

The handcuffs broke. Screaming like a beast, he slammed his numb arms against the heads of his captors. Blood sprayed onto the car's windows.

Outside the car, he saw other cars, trucks, the fronts of shops. Even as he reached for the driver's head, the car accelerated. The driver twisted from Lyons' grasp. His fingers were too numb to grab the man's hair. Lyons thrust himself forward, hooked his arm around the man's throat, pulled him backwards with incredible force.

The car swerved out of control. A pistol's blast seared the air around him. With Lyons' one arm still around the driver's throat, the other arm hammering into the bloody face of the Oriental with the pistol, the car leaped the curb and crashed.

Now, amidst battered, grappling people, Lyons had the pistol. He fell backwards from the open door, rolling onto the sidewalk. Faces peered down at him.

"Police officer!" Lyons screamed. *"Stand back! Back!"* He stood gasping, sucking air into his lungs. The crowd gathering around him stared. A woman looked away, covered her mouth. Two small kids carrying shopping bags gaped at him, their mouths open. One kid said to the other, "That cop's all messed up. Betcha he dies."

Lyons wiped his face, saw blood and flesh on his hand. He felt the back of his head, found a quite small sore spot, but no wound. Had they pistol-whipped him? Hit him with a blackjack? No time to speculate. He stood up gingerly.

The Orientals' car was a late-model Ford sedan. It had taken off the left front fender of a parked Volkswagen, jumped the curb, snapped off a parking meter, crashed into a telephone pole. Lyons had apparently kicked out a rear door window. There was a neat hole in the roof where a bullet had exited.

Lyons glanced into the front seat and saw a young Oriental woman with blood on her face, lying in the footwell. She wore a conservative blue skirt-suit with a white silk blouse and knotted scarf. Her skirt was up around her thighs, exposing long slim legs. A garter holster held a .22 automatic just above one knee.

Lyons kept the captured pistol pointed at her head, took the .22 automatic, then slipped his hand under her jacket. She wore another pistol in a shoulder holster. Again, an automatic. He pocketed the second pistol. Suddenly she tried to jab her fingers into his eyes, but he jammed his pistol into her solar plexus. She gagged, choked.

Beyond her in the front seat, the driver was dead, his neck broken. The other two moved. One breathed through a mangled mouth and jaw. Blood and pieces of teeth spilled down his shirt. His jaw twisted oddly to one side. The other was unconscious, but alive. Blood flowed from scalp wounds. The Orientals' slacks and shirts were splotched with blood.

"Officer? Officer?" A shopkeeper in a denim apron came up to Lyons. "Should I call for an ambulance? Would you like to use our phone?"

"My backup is on the way."

"Your backup is here." Gadgets ran up to Lyons, and winced when he saw the blood all over him. Gadgets still had the Uzi concealed beneath his satchel. "Are you okay? Why don't you sit down? I'll take over."

"I'm okay. Where'd you come from?"

"You're only a block and half from the building. Blancanales is back. He's okay. Now siddown, you're a mess!"

"It's not *my* blood, all this, it's theirs. Help me wrap it up. Take these pistols. I need to find my .357."

Lyons dumped the captured pistols into Gadgets' satchel, then searched through the car. He found his .357 Magnum and the .38 revolvers he had captured from the Puerto Rican sentries. He found the hand-radio, pressed the transit button.

"*Numero Uno* Badass here, come in *Numero Dos.*" Lyons buzzed the transmit button a few more times, then heard Blancanales' reply: "This is your worried friend. I'm in the garage. Where are you?"

"Stick tight, we'll be there in a flash. Wait till you see what I got for you. Very interesting." Lyons turned to Gadgets. "Get in the back. I'm taking these losers back to where we can ask them some questions."

Waiting in the alley, Blancanales saw a Ford with a smashed front make a turn, accelerate toward him. For an instant, as the car approached, he didn't recognize the driver. The man's face was smeared with clots of blood. But then Lyons grinned, and Blancanales pointed into the garage. He waited until his partners were inside the building, then spoke into his hand-radio. "Taximan? You still parked? This is Badman Number Two."

"Yes, sir. Parked and waiting. What do you need?"

"Come around the block, park in front of the garage. Let us know if anyone interesting shows up."

"Yes sir. In motion now."

"Slow down. We've got it under control. Where's Smith? What's he doing?"

"He followed that florist's truck out to Brooklyn. Sir, I've been getting a lot of calls from the agents around the Tower. They want to know what's going on with you three. Things are very tense back there."

"Tell them there's been a major break in the investigation. I'll be bringing them a folder full of names and faces. Things are moving fast." Blancanales looked into the garage, saw Lyons pulling a struggling young woman out of the Ford. "In fact, things might be out of control. Over."

The dark-haired young woman in the skirt-suit hammered at Lyons with a high-heeled shoe. She broke away from Lyons and Gadgets and ran for the open door to the alley.

Blancanales grabbed the rolling door's chain, pulled the door down. Her escape blocked, she stopped, looked at her captors, her eyes moving like a trapped animal's. She sprinted in another direction. Lyons ran after her.

He chased her into a corner. As he approached, the woman—standing about five foot two without her shoes—took a kung-fu stance and clenched her fists, waiting for him. Lyons went into the shotokan karate sparring stance, but kept his hands at his sides. When he was very close to her, he twitched one shoulder as a feint.

She jumped straight up, shot a side kick at his throat.

Lyons caught her ankle with one hand and dragged her in one sweeping movement across the concrete to the other prisoners. She shrieked, clawed at him, cursed in her language. Lyons stepped on her throat and passed two of the plastic handcuffs to Blancanales.

"Hands and feet. Cinch her up tight. This one is hardcore."

"You got it," Blancanales told Lyons, "I haven't seen one like her for ten years."

As Blancanales pulled the plastic loops tight around her ankles and wrists, he spoke to the young woman in her language. She didn't answer. Gadgets came over, spoke also. She looked from man to man, and finally said, "Your Vietnamese is very poor. I would rather speak English."

"Vietnamese?" Lyons was incredulous. Despite his aching skull, the strong-jawed man stared quietly at the girl. "How'd you people get involved in this?"

"That's what I asked her," Blancanales told him.

"Who are you?" Lyons demanded.

"I am Le Van Thanh, of the People's Army of Vietnam."

The three men stared at her.

"You do not believe me?" She spoke textbook English, very correctly, as if in a language class.

"Long way from home, aren't you?" Lyons queried.

"Other representatives of my government attempted to speak to your officials, and they, too, were not believed. Your government displayed an overwhelming hostility, despite our good intentions. May I sit up, please?"

Blancanales pulled her up so that she could lean back against the Ford. She laid her head back against the door, exhausted. In her tailored, conservative blue skirt-suit, she looked like a young bank executive.

"If you had such good intentions," Lyons asked, "how come you put a pistol up against my head? How come you kidnapped me?"

"I was not responsible for that blunder!" Le Van Thanh looked at the Oriental with the broken jaw. "My superior has a very different attitude toward Americans than I do. He thought it better to capture you, interrogate you, before we discussed our mutual concerns."

"What mutual concerns?" Lyons demanded.

Blancanales interrupted. "Wait. How did you know who this officer is—" he indicated Lyons "—and where he would be?"

"We have contacts with the *Fuerzas*—you call them the FALN. Our contacts told us there would be a conference between the local commander of their organization and a federal officer. They told us it would be possible for our group also to speak with that officer. But it was imperative that the *Fuerza* commander not know of our group's involvement.

"We meant to wait for your officer's return to this location, then speak with him. However, the meeting did not occur exactly as anticipated. My superior misjudged the situation. He decided to take one of the secondary officers—you," she pointed to Lyons. "My superior meant to interrogate you, then offer information concerning our mutual problem if you federal officers would cooperate. We meant you no harm. We carried a special electronic stun device so as to. . . ."

"A Taser!" Gadgets reached under the Ford's seat, brought out the plastic pistol. "Fifty thousand volts," he said admiringly. "Quite a shock, knocks most people down."

"I thought you'd shot me in the head," Lyons told the woman. "I thought I was dying."

"That would have defeated our purpose. We wanted cooperation, not death."

"What is this cooperation you want?" Blancanales asked.

"First, I will tell you the information. It is this. An individual of Puerto Rican ancestry approached our government for aid in his organization's struggle against your government. This individual claimed to represent the FALN. In truth, he did not. Our government explained to that individual that the People's Republic of Vietnam hoped for better relations with the United States of America. Furnishing war material to dissident organizations would not be conducive to normal relations between our nations. Therefore, the request was denied."

"By war material, you mean C-4 explosives and M-16 rifles?" Lyons asked.

"Yes, explosives and weapons."

"But you say you didn't give it to him? Then where did they get the material?"

"Our government did not supply the explosives and weapons. But he may indeed have purchased the material in our country. You know our land is in turmoil. War creates many vices. And our nation has had many generations of war. He offered our government gold. When we refused, perhaps he found those who did not hesitate.''

''And that's the information?'' Lyons asked.

''Why did you want to tell us about this?'' Blancanales sighed. ''Why not the people in Washington, D.C.?''

''We did. I told you they did not believe us. Also, they would not consider cooperation with our group.''

''Thank you for the information,'' Blancanales sighed. ''Now, explain what 'cooperation' you want from us.''

''It is simply this. The individual and his group have deceived and embarrassed our government. They could seriously impair our nation's future relations with your nation. We assume you will eventually capture these...terrorists. You will?''

''Pretty quick,'' Lyons told her.

''We want them exterminated. No investigation. No trials. No public revelations. Could that be arranged?''

The three members of the Able Team glanced at one another. Lyons frowned. ''Do you have more information on the individual who approached your government? And the other terrorists?'' he asked.

''Photographs, notes,'' she replied.

''Show us.''

''The information is not in the automobile. We have a rented apartment in this city. Would you take me there? I could give....''

''We'll discuss this,'' Blancanales interrupted. He

glanced at Lyons and Gadgets. "Conference time."

They went to a far corner of the garage. Blancanales covered the young woman where she sat against the car.

"What do you two think?" Lyons asked them. "You both know Vietnamese people better than I do."

"That woman is one of the smartest people I ever ran up against," Gadgets told them. "And I know, *I know*, it isn't the way she says."

"It's lies inside of lies," Blancanales concurred. "But you'd better believe they want those people dead. Exterminated."

"We need the information she's talking about," Lyons told them. "I want the photos. I want the notes. Even when we do get the psychos inside the Tower, that won't mean we've got their *leaders*."

"Right," Blancanales said. "I've got a folder full of punks and crazies, but none among them is the mastermind."

Inside the satchel slung over Gadgets' shoulder, a hand-radio buzzed. "Hardman Three here," he responded.

"Mr. Taxi relaying a message." All of them could hear the voice coming from the hand-radio. "There's a man named Brognola screaming for you all. He says to get back to the Tower, *right now*. I mean, he is pissed. Over."

Lyons keyed the hand-radio. "Tell him we're coming back real quick. Tell him there's been significant progress."

"Things must be critical over there," Gadgets said. "But so is this."

"Okay, you two go back," Lyons offered. "I'll go with her."

"I can send back my info with Gadgets," Blancanales countered. "You'll need backup if you're going to find out what she's talking about."

"You two be careful now," Gadgets warned. "That chick is dangerous."

Lyons checked his watch. Thirty-six hours remaining. "Five o'clock, gentlemen. Time sure flies when you're having fun."

10

On the fifty-third floor of the World Financial Corporation Tower, in the offices of Eastern European Accounts, the afternoon went very slowly. Charlie Green, as reluctant commander of his office staff, prepared the women to defend themselves if the terrorists came to their floor.

First, he went to the custodian's closet and kicked down the door. He found a few tools, a set of master keys for the floor, and coveralls. He stripped off his running clothes and slipped on the coveralls. If the terrorists got him, he didn't want them to think he was an executive. The coveralls also gave him pockets for the .45 automatic and the tools and keys.

Opening an office near the elevators, he posted Diane as sentry. She seemed to be the coolest of the three young women. He placed her so that she had maximum concealment and safety. "Sit in here, keep the door open only two or three inches, and watch those elevators. If anybody, I mean, *anybody*—crazies, police, phone company, security guards—comes out on this floor, you let out a scream, then close this door. They'll have to break it down. That'll warn us. I'll be back in a few minutes to work out an escape plan for you."

"You mean they get me so that you others can get

away?'' Diane asked sarcastically. ''I think you ought to get another volunteer.''

''Only for awhile,'' he assured her. ''Then we'll have a better plan in operation.''

Green returned to the other women. As the director of the department, Green had the largest office on this floor. There was a large work area for clerks and computer workers, a reception area with Mrs. Forde's desk, then his private office.

''Jill,'' he told the terrified young woman in thick glasses, ''go to the janitor's room. The door's open. There's a dolly for moving furniture in there. Bring it here. Sandy, go to my office and tear down the drapes. Separate the nylon cord from the hardware, coil it up.'' Green waited until the young women left the office.

''Now, Mrs. Forde,'' he said, turning to her last. ''We plan an ambush.''

For the next half hour, they moved filing cabinets, shifted furniture, improvised booby-traps. Green briefed each woman on her role. ''It's not necessary for us to kill them all. We don't have to kill any of them. We'll just give them a surprise, and that'll slow them down while we retreat. These three offices will be surprise number one. Then we go up into the ceiling and into the other offices. And the more time they give us before they come searching this floor, the more surprises we'll have ready for them....''

Leaving Mrs. Forde in charge of the ''surprise,'' Green roamed through the other offices of the fifty-third floor. He ripped down drapes, pasted sheets of computer printout against the plate glass. He wanted the police to know people were trapped on the floor.

Perhaps rescue was possible. But he doubted they could be rescued before the police recaptured the Tower.

In fact, it was with some relief that he doubted the value of any preparations to avoid the terrorists. The Tower had a hundred floors, a thousand offices, many thousands of rooms and cubicles. If the terrorists had hostages to guard, police to watch, demands to negotiate, they wouldn't have time to search the Tower. There would have to be a hundred terrorists.

The preparations were busy-work, for the women and for him. Panic was their greatest enemy. If he gave the women plans to remember and positions to hold, they would have less time to be afraid.

He knew from his tours in Vietnam that waiting created fear. When trouble came, it came fast. It was life or death. But in the hours or days or months of waiting, the imagination created terrors. He'd had some bad times over there, but some of the worst times were the nights without action, without contact, when there was only darkness and fear and imagination.

Finding a transistor radio in one of the offices, he started back to the women. He paused to test Diane. Part of the "surprise" was her new position as sentry. She sat in the corridor where she could watch all the elevators. If anyone were to come onto the floor, either from the elevators or from the emergency stairs at each end of the corridor, she was to run into the office, set the plan in action.

She saw him, started, but recognized him before she gave a false alarm. "You trying to scare me?" she asked, giggling nervously.

"Take a break," he told her. "Switch with Jill or Sandy. Time to listen to the news."

Back in his office, Green scanned the rooftops of the nearby buildings. Almost invisible in the shadows of a building's air-conditioning stacks, a black-clad sniper waited. "That's the police," said Green with assurance.

Switching on the radio, he spun the dial. But they heard no reports of terrorists on Wall Street, or of shots fired at executives, or of a hostage drama in the financial district.

"Don't they know what's happening to us?" Jill asked. "Are they keeping it a secret? What's going on down there that they have to keep it a secret from everyone?"

Green sat her down in his desk chair. "Calm, kiddo. Be cool. Nothing secret's going on. Why don't you stay here at the window and let us know what happens down there? Just watch, okay?"

It would be a long afternoon. He knew he could keep his staff calm for a few more hours; but what if the siege went on into the night? What if the terrorists cut the lights in the upper floors? What if the terrorists came searching for them in the pitch darkness of a blacked-out Tower? Who would keep *him* calm?

In the second-floor office of Tower security, Zuniga listened to a federal agent speaking calmly and patiently of negotiation. He leaned back in the swivel chair, held the phone's hand-set away from his ear. The voice droned on.

"With the Puerto Rican elections so close," the

agent reminded him, "do you think an incident like this will promote your cause? Your own sympathizers might support your action, but what of the millions of Puerto Ricans who are not so certain in their opinions? We should resolve this incident quickly, before something unfortunate turns those millions of your people against you. Your seizure of the Corporation's Tower will give you international publicity, that's for sure, but...."

Operating through a different circuit and switcher from the other phone lines serving the Tower, the security office's line remained open because neither Zuniga's squad nor the police had cut it. Ana had been trained to jam the building's main switcher without destroying it. She had later bypassed the jamming to test for outside interference. All the lines were now jammed from the outside also. Zuniga was sure that if he attempted to call out, the number and conversation would be monitored. But that did not disturb him. Communication with his leader was unnecessary.

"...loss of life and terror won't help your cause with other nations. After all, the United States has anti-terrorist treaties with most of the nations of the world, even Cuba and the Soviet Union."

Zuniga's walkie-talkie buzzed. He covered the phone's mouthpiece, keyed the walkie-talkie. "Squad leader here."

"Calling from the lobby. We have movement in the plaza."

"Watch them. I'll be there soon." Then he spoke into the telephone. "This is what we want. I'll repeat it again. One, freedom for Puerto Rico. Two, freedom for all Puerto Ricans in the jails and prisons of the fascist Federal States of America. Three, a ticker-tape parade for myself and my squad!"

Laughing, Zuniga slammed down the phone, left the security office. He took the elevator up one floor to the auditorium. There, Julio watched the doors of the auditorium, from time to time unlocking the doors to glance inside.

"Any problems?" Zuniga asked him.

Julio laughed. "Crying and screaming. People begging me."

"Any of them try to make a break?"

"I wish!" Julio caressed the steel and black fiberglass of his M-16. "You see that fat man I greased? Just like someone dropped a bagful of shit and guts. All over the floor."

"Anyone give you trouble, wait until I come up. We'll do something interesting."

"What?"

"There's a stage in there, right? We'll make an example of them. Give the Yankees something to watch."

Going down to the first floor, Zuniga saw Rico scanning the plaza surrounding the Tower, standing exposed to view. The squad had no fear of federal snipers. Zuniga had warned the agents watching the Tower that shooting one of his soldiers would mean death to ten hostages.

"There," Rico pointed as Zuniga joined him. "They moved from the barricade to those bushes. One of them carried something."

He took Rico's binoculars, focused the four-power lenses on a hedge a hundred yards past the plate glass of the lobby. Zuniga could not see a face, but there was a silhouette visible through the pattern of the branches and leaves.

"Do I shoot him?" Rico asked.

"Wait. Watch him. Call me if he moves again."

Zuniga keyed his walkie-talkie three times. Ana answered him. "Are you finished?" he asked her.

"Almost. A few more."

Below him, in the cavernous first parking level, Ana and Luisa worked to protect the squad from surprise assault. In the first minutes of the takeover, Ana had placed claymores to guard the squad's rear as they moved into the Tower. But those claymores were "quickies," as Zuniga called them. Now, they placed a second set of anti-personnel devices, following diagrams Zuniga had prepared in the months of planning for the takeover.

The diagrams indicated the placement of each claymore and bomb, the monofilament trip-lines or pressure-triggers, and the kill zones. The positions were numbered on the diagrams to correspond to the tags on the preassembled and individually packed devices. Zuniga knew at the outset that he would not have the soldiers to guard the parking level's street entrances. He knew also that his soldiers' limited training could not match the expertise of the New York City and FBI bomb squads. Zuniga had left nothing to chance.

He went down to the parking level to inspect their work. Ana accompanied him, pointing out each claymore or bomb, and its trigger. His planning and preparation had allowed Ana and Luisa to move quickly, simply removing each device from its container, then putting it in position.

Claymores guarded the rollaway steel doors blocking the entrance from the street. Aimed to spray thousands of glass beads across the entry, the triggers were nearly invisible strands of monofilament. One claymore would explode if someone tripped over the monofilament. But the second and third would not: the second would explode if the monofilament trigger were cut, so any officer attempting to defuse the device would be killed or dismembered. The third claymore, though on the same monofilament trigger, would not explode until three minutes later, perhaps killing other officers who came to the aid of the wounded or dying.

Zuniga had packed the claymores with glass beads because glass, unlike lead or steel, is invisible to X rays. Any officer wounded would suffer the rest of his life.

Throughout the vast garage, strands of monofilament criss-crossed the concrete. Some strands were at ankle height, others at chest height. Some trigger strands were false, only there to confuse and delay a defusing team. But many strands led to claymores.

Near the elevator doors, a thin electrical wire led from a rubber mat to a detonator set in half a kilo of C-4. But the wire was dead, and the detonator a fake. The C-4 charge would explode only if the fake detonator were pulled from the charge.

At the doors to the stairways leading up to the lobby, claymores had been placed in the pipes and wiring in the ceiling. But the devices were not triggered by tightly stretched monofilament. Instead, many tiny three-barbed fish hooks hung at waist height on transparent nylon wire. If an officer brushed past the hooks, the hooks would catch in his clothing and trigger the claymore. On the other side of the door, there were simple pull-triggers: if someone pulled open the door, he died.

As a final touch to frustrate the defusing teams, Ana and Luisa scattered bits of C-4 explosive. On the concrete, under the few parked cars, in the drains, in the recesses of the concrete ceiling. A dog trained to sniff out explosives would smell C-4 everywhere.

Their work pleased Zuniga. The two young women had secured the Tower against attack from below. Zuniga had often had discipline problems with the women in the months of rehearsal, but the thrill of their role—knowing they might kill or dismember many police officers—drove the young women on through the long hours of lessons. And now another force drove them. Fear. If the police succeeded in storming the Tower, the squad faced death or capture. And capture meant the living death of life in the high-security prisons of the enemy.

"Excellent! Excellent!" he told them.

Luisa laughed. "If the pigs try to get through here, I'm gonna come down and take a look, after it's all over."

"Now the lobby," Zuniga told them. He punched the elevator's up button. "And when you're done there, we'll put together a special surprise for our hostages. For when they escape."

The doors slid closed. In the privacy of the elevator, he allowed himself a smile. The plan was progressing smoothly. In the first few hours of the siege, they had accomplished all their objectives. They had cut the building's communications. They had placed the explosives and incendiaries. They had captured the corporation's employees. The squad would soon be safe from police attack. The only threat to the plan was the shattering of the radio-detonator when Ana lost her pistol to the man in the jogging suit. But the loss of the detonator would not be a problem. The "escape" of the employees would trigger the charges.

11

Blood-red water swirled over the white enamel of the sink. Lyons scrubbed the clotted blood of the Vietnamese off his face as he talked with Blancanales in the washroom of the garage.

"She could give us the link between the creeps in the WorldFiCor tower," Lyons argued, "and the main man, the number one creep who set it all up."

"Let the feds pump her full of chemicals," Blancanales countered. "Then we'll go check out her group's apartment. I smell trap all over this."

"Any blood on my back?" Lyons asked, trying to peer over his shoulder into the mirror.

"There's blood all over you," Blancanales said. He dabbed at splotches on Lyons' suitcoat. "The inside of that car looked like a grenade went off. Bet that's the last time they ever think of kidnapping an American."

Lyons held up the broken handcuffs to Blancanales. "What's that say on there?"

"Made in the People's Republic of Vietnam."

"Cheap imitations," Lyons scoffed. "Thing is, there's no way she could have contacted her people—if there are any others. When I walk in there with her, I've got them cold. I'll take an Uzi, a tear-gas grenade, all the standard stuff. She pulls any trash,

I'll gas them and blast my way out. I'm on a winning streak today—can't lose!''

Blancanales laughed. "If you say so."

A siren sounded, startling them. Lyons looked into the auto shop area, saw the ambulance with the three Vietnamese pulling away. Le Van Thanh waited with Mr. Taxi and Mr. Smith, liaison agents for the Able Team.

Lyons dried his hands and face with a white shop towel. Then he folded the towel, moistened one corner of it. "For her. She's got blood on her, too."

"So courteous," Blancanales joked. "Next thing you'll be taking her handcuffs off."

"No way. What I figure is that with her group a complete failure, she can't go back to Vietnam. So she wants to cut a deal with us. Hoping she won't go to prison. Makes sense?"

"None of this makes sense."

Lyons and Le Van Thanh went ahead in the taxi. Blancanales followed with Mr. Smith. Even as the afternoon faded, the day's heat intensified. On the sidewalks, girls in gauze dresses and sheer summer tops ignored the smiles and quips of men on apartment steps. Kids sprinted through sprays of water. Ice cream vendors pushed their carts home, all sold out.

Le Van Thanh rode in the back seat of the taxi with Lyons, her hands cuffed in front of her, her ankles cuffed too. After she had managed to wipe the blood from her face, Lyons had found a brush for her. She was a beautiful young woman, but her face was set in an impassive mask. Lyons wondered idly if it was fear or fanaticism. But it didn't really matter to him.

He had Gadgets' bag full of Uzi death. If the Vietnamese woman made one wrong move, he'd empty a magazine through her.

But if she helped him save the lives of the World-FiCor employees captured in the Tower, he'd go to every office in Washington D.C. to plead her case. And if there was any truth in the story she had told him, that made her an ally against terrorism. Besides, she was pretty and had a dangerously high kick. He'd like to take her to a disco.

The FBI cabbie watched the streets pass, then turned at last into a quiet street of brownstone apartments. They were old apartments with new paint, contemporary windows, security entries. Cadillacs and Porsches and Saabs lined the curbs.

"Good neighborhood," Lyons commented.

"The building with the blue door," she told the FBI cabbie. She turned to Lyons, holding up her cuffed wrists. "How can I go in with these chains?"

"You don't need to go in. Wait here."

"If I don't go in, you must kill the soldier in the apartment. But if I do go in, I can tell him to surrender. Then we will take the files and leave. It will only take two minutes."

Lyons glanced through the taxi's rear window. Smith and Blancanales pulled to the curb behind them.

"Taximan."

"Yes, sir."

"Last-minute conference with my partner," Lyons told him. "Take out your weapon, don't turn your back on her. She makes a move before I get back, kill her." Lyons looked to Le Van Thanh. "You understand?"

"You must think me very foolish. I, a chained foreigner in a strange city, guarded by several men with weapons, should try to escape?"

"So don't."

He glanced to the roofs of the apartment buildings, to the windows of the apartments overlooking the street. He saw no one watching the street. Down the block, an elderly woman walked a poodle.

With the canvas bag's strap over his shoulder, and the Uzi concealed in the bag, Lyons left the taxi cautiously. He'd already made one mistake today. He gripped the Uzi, his finger on the trigger, thumb on the safety. He scanned the roof lines again as he walked back to the other car.

Blancanales had equipment spread out over the back seat, with a newspaper folded out to conceal it all from pedestrians' view. Lyons got in the front seat.

"She says there's a soldier in there. Said if I don't take her in with me, I'll have to shoot it out with the man."

"It's your decision," Blancanales told him.

"Great. Wait till I'm in the building with her, then follow us in. Smith," he turned to the federal agent. "I want you to keep a channel open to your people and the police."

"Backup?" Smith asked.

"Whatever happens will happen too fast for backup. We'll just pull out and leave them to pick up the pieces, explain things to the neighbors. I'm on my way."

On the sidewalk again, he watched for curtains moving, for neighborhood people, for any movement at all. Nothing. Only the distant music of radios, the rush of traffic on the avenue. He got into the taxi.

"All right," Lyons told her. "You and I go in."

He leaned down and unlocked the cuffs on her ankles. She held up her wrists. He shook his head.

"You are one dangerous lady." He stepped out of the taxi, holding the door open for her. Staring straight ahead, she left the taxi, walking quickly to the entry of the apartment house she had pointed out. Lyons watched her long, slim legs flash from the banker-blue of her long skirt. He hadn't noticed the slits at the sides of her skirt before.

That's a good sign, he thought. *Fashionable young women don't die for a cause.*

Half-running to catch up with her, he took her keys from his pocket, opened the door with his left hand. Fashionable skirt or not, he kept his right hand on the Uzi.

Inside, he saw a rubber doorstop. As Le Van Thanh walked to the elevator, Lyons kicked the doorstop to the threshold, pulled the door closed against it. The door remained open half an inch. It took only a second. Then he went to the elevator, pulled her away as the doors slid open.

"We'll take the stairs."

"But it is four floors up."

"You're healthy, you can do it. You first. Fast!"

She hurried up the four flights of stairs, Lyons a few steps behind her. Was she swaying her hips deliberately? Or was the supple sway just natural to her?

In the narrow, closed stairwell, he became aware of her perfume and sweat.

At the fourth floor fire door, she stopped and turned to him. "Helping you makes me a traitor to my country. I can never return. Will you help me? I will cooperate with you." She stepped closer to him, her mask of fear or fanaticism gone, her face vulnerable, her eyes searching his face for a response. She stepped closer, her small breasts almost touching him as her chest rose and fell with her breathing.

"I will cooperate completely," she pleaded, promised. "In any way you want. But save me, your government is so cruel. They will show me no pity when. . . ."

As she snapped her knee into his groin, Lyons whipped his hips sideways to her, blocked her knee with his own. He tried to block her fists with his left hand, took her double-hand blow to his stomach, fell back against the stair rail.

Screaming in Vietnamese, she jerked open the fire door and ran into the hallway. Lyons bounced off the railing. He pressed himself against the stairwell wall next to the door, reaching for the hand-radio in his left-hand coat pocket.

But it got too noisy to speak. Slugs splintered the fire door, hammering plaster from the opposite wall. Burst after burst ripped through the door, at chest height, then at knee height, slugs gouging into the landing's linoleum.

Watching the ragged holes appearing in the door, and the sudden holes in the wall and floor, Lyons calculated where the gunman stood on the other side of the door. He waited until at least thirty shots had come through, then, betting his life that it was an AK-47 with a thirty-round magazine pointed at him, he stepped away from the wall, and fired waist-high through the door.

The stream of 9mm slugs swept the hallway the other side of the door. Lyons didn't need to open the fire door to see what he had done. Through a splinter-framed hole, he saw a blood-splashed wall and a young Vietnamese man on the floor, clutching his chest.

Lyons jerked open the door. The dead youth stared at the ceiling, his fingers knotted into the bloody mess of his chest. At his side was an AK-47 without the magazine. A full magazine lay on the hallway's carpet, in the rapidly spreading pool of blood.

Past the dead boy, Lyons saw only a window at the end of the hall. Le Van Thanh was gone.

"Politician!" Lyons called out. "You there?"

"Elevator!" said a hoarse whisper.

"The kid with the AK is dead. You see the woman?"

"She made it into this apartment."

Lunging across the wide hallway, Lyons snatched the AK-47 and the full magazine. Both rifle and magazine were slick with blood. He jammed in the magazine, chambered a round, wiped off the weapon with his coat sleeve.

AK-47 in his left hand, Uzi in his right, he crept back to the elevator. At the closed door to the apartment opposite the elevator he glanced back. Blancanales watched him from the elevator, pointed at the door, made a fist. Lyons nodded.

The AK-47 jumping awkwardly in his one-hand grip, Lyons fired bursts into the hinges and lock, then emptied the magazine through the door. Blancanales ran from the elevator, went to one knee, waited.

Suddenly, shots came from the apartment, punching into the wall by the elevator.

Lyons kicked the splintered door down, threw the AK-47 through the doorway, heard it crash into furniture. Both Lyons and Blancanales fired crisscrossing bursts into the apartment.

Blancanales dived through the doorway, low, as Lyons fired over him. He heard Blancanales exchanging fire, shots hitting the wall, breaking glass. Furniture crashed. Lyons glanced in, saw Blancanales roll behind an overstuffed velvet couch as a Vietnamese man shouldered an AK, firing a burst. Then the Vietnamese saw Lyons, and turned.

Lyons ducked back as shots ripped wood from the door frame beside his face. Then he heard the Uzi burst. The AK fire went wild. A man screamed.

Lyons looked again. The Vietnamese was gone, the window behind where he had stood was gone. The afternoon breeze flagged the curtains.

A pistol shot roared past Lyons' ear. He dropped, heard another pistol shot rip over him, then the Uzi fired again. Blancanales would be out of ammo by now. Lyons fired from the floor, rolling into the apartment. He saw Le Van Thanh aiming a pistol down at him, her hands still chained together. Lyons fired.

The first slug punched into the wall behind her, but the second and third hit her shoulder, threw bits of flesh and cloth onto the wall, and spun her violently around. She dropped to the floor. The pistol clattered against the wall. Lyons took aim at her head, but his gun was empty.

Incredibly, she came up with an AK. She watched Lyons grappling with Gadgets' satchel, trying to get the Uzi out. Meanwhile he was watching the wounded woman drop the empty magazine from the AK and try to snap in another. But with one hand on the grip, and the handcuffs still linking her wrists, she couldn't quite reach the AK's cocking lever.

Making a quick decision, he swung the satchel by its shoulder strap, the nylon bag heavy with Uzi and magazines, hand-radio and spent brass, coming down on her head hard, stunning her. She dropped the AK. Lyons swung the satchel again, saw blood gushing from her head, pouring over her face and white blouse.

Still she struggled, putting her hands out in front of her in kung-fu claws, kicking, but in the slow motion of semi-consciousness. Lyons dropped the satchel, took out his Colt Python .357, grabbed her by her lustrous black hair, smashed her in the ear with the Python's heavy barrel.

Silence. Lyons looked around, saw Blancanales jump up, kick open a door. Nothing. Blancanales looked into the room, then went in. He came out in a moment, giving Lyons the thumbs up.

Blancanales crossed the apartment, glanced into another room, searched through a closet, finally came back to Lyons. He looked down at the bleeding woman.

"She alive?"

"Sure she's alive! She's alive 'cause she has a date with interrogation. The men with hypodermics. Then she'll explain what this is all about."

He looked around the apartment again, surveying the damage.

It had been a spacious apartment with French windows overlooking the trees of the street. Now most of the glass was shot out. One entire window was gone. The curtains were sprayed with blood. The furnishings were ripped, broken, overturned, dusted with plaster and bits of brick. The velvet couch looked as if it had been attacked with a chain saw. Lines of automatic rounds dotted the walls, huge hunks of plaster broken away from the bricks underneath.

"See what happens when you rent to foreigners?" Lyons asked Blancanales. "They have no respect for things. It lowers the property values."

Blancanales laughed. He changed magazines on his Uzi. "Come into this other room, take a look."

A bedroom had been converted into an intelligence office. Tables were stacked with papers and photos. Row after row of eight-by-ten black-and-white glossies were pinned to the wall.

"Is the war over?" Taximan called from the hallway. "Where are you?"

"In here," Lyons called.

"See those photos?" Blancanales pointed to one series. "Recognize the crazies from that folder I have? The FALN information? These Vietnamese were onto the group."

Taximan came in. "We got to get out of here. There's a crowd outside, the police are on their way. We got a Vietnamese hanging out of a tree with most of his head gone. I'm afraid this is going to be on the six o'clock news.''

Lyons didn't listen. He studied a series of photos. In one photo, the man the FALN folder identified as both a terrorist and embezzler spoke with a young man. In another photo, the unidentified young man spoke with an older man. Though the photo was grainy black and white, taken with a telephoto lens, Lyons recognized the distinguished sandy-haired gentleman talking with the hard-faced young man. He had seen the gentleman posing with a former President and Secretary of State. He was the President of the World Financial Corporation.

12

Siren wailing, a New York Police Department squad car cut through the late-afternoon traffic. Taximan kept the front bumper of the cab only a few car lengths behind the police black-and-white, roaring through intersections at sixty miles an hour, throwing the wheel from side to side to swerve around slow trucks, accelerating in open stretches of avenue, power-gliding around corners.

In the cab's back seat, Lyons shouted instructions through the security phone. "I want a team of sur-veillance agents ready *right now*! Street clothes, unmarked cars, panel trucks. They'll need hand-radios, D.F.'s, minimikes. Cameras with light inten-sification lenses, super-fast film. And I want an M-16 with a Starlite scope. I want them ready to move when we get there, and we're on our way in, *now*!"

He shared the backseat with Blancanales and sev-eral boxes of photos and paperwork taken from the apartment. Blancanales patiently sorted through the material as the cab skidded from side to side of the streets and avenues. He skimmed over the typed and handwritten Vietnamese, a language in which he was fluent, searching for names. There were hun-dreds of sheets.

"Anything?" Lyons asked.

"It'll take me weeks to get through all this. But look at these dates, they go back months. This was no rush job. They've been on it quite a while."

"Any background? Why they were sent? What they were looking for?"

"Can't tell. These are only day-to-day logs. Surveillance records. Copies of weekly reports. All signed by Le Van Thanh."

"She was the commander?"

"That's right. When they stitch her head back together, we'll have to ask her about Davis and that other man, the man who links Davis to the crazies. I see Davis' name all over the place, but I don't see the go-between's. Maybe they didn't get it."

"What is the hold the crazies have on Davis?" Lyons pondered the mystery out loud. Then, to Blancanales: "When did the crazies first contact him? You find anything that could tell us that? What's the date on the first picture with the go-between and Davis?"

"The photos aren't dated." He held up one eight-by-ten. "Labels with numbers. The numbers refer to reports. But I haven't matched up the reports yet with the photos. Can't until I have some help with this."

"Then they could have been talking to Davis for a week, two weeks?"

"Could be they had pressure on him before the Vietnamese came to New York. We could go straight to Davis. With these photos, he can't deny meeting with the crazies."

"He could have told me this morning, and he didn't. Maybe they have his children or grandchildren, and he thinks he can tough it out on his own. Maybe they've been threatening his company all along. Maybe taking the Tower was only the final turn of the screw. I want Davis watched. Because whatever they want from him, now's the time to take it. And when they try, we'll take their contact man.''

Federal agents in electrical company uniforms watched the squad car and taxi roar past, then replaced the street barricades. In seconds, the cab screeched to a smoking-tire stop.

''Just take the photos with Davis in it,'' Lyons told Blancanales. ''We'll have these agents carry the boxes in. They're just hanging around anyway. Heard what I said, Taximan?''

''I'll put them to work, sir. Right away.''

They ran from the cab, weaving through the agents in uniforms and street clothes standing at the commandeered office building's back entrance. An agent at the glass doors stopped them.

''Who are you guys? Show me some official identification.''

''We don't have identification,'' Lyons told him, tried to shove past. The agent shoved back, and found himself on his back on the concrete, looking up at Lyons and Blancanales.

Blancanales laughed, put his hand on Lyons' shoulder. ''Ease up, man. These guys are on our side!''

An agent in gray janitor coveralls stepped from the building and held the door open for them.

''I'm Hardman Three's liaison man,'' he said. ''He's waiting for you upstairs. Many interesting developments.''

Another man—slight-figured, in a conservative suit and brown shoes, carrying a zippered folder—rushed to the door of the elevator. But Lyons straight-armed him, said, "Wait for the next one up."

"Please," Blancanales added.

"But he's..." the liaison agent protested. The elevator doors closed. The car shot up. "He was waiting to talk to you. He has some background material on WorldFiCor."

Lyons turned to the agent, emphasized his words with a finger to the man's chest. "I want you to understand this, Mr. Agent. We have been in the shit all day long. We have done the work you feds can't. And the reason we can do it is that we don't exist. We don't have identification, we don't have names. You have never seen us. We will never be news, we will never be on TV. No one will ever include us in their exposé, or in their memoirs. If we get killed, we're just meat in a body-bag, no name and no face. So we show up here, and what do we have? Some clerk with a notebook trying to brief us. That is a violation of our working rules! When Brognola tells me to talk to the man, then I talk to him, not before. Nobody comes up and introduces himself to us! Do you understand?"

"Right. Yes, sir. Mr. Brognola has to give you the okay. I'll call him back, right now. Security is important."

"You talked to Brognola?" Blancanales asked.

The elevator stopped, and Lyons stepped out as the doors slid open. He glanced in both directions down the corridor, but all the doors were closed.

"Yes, sir. He called me." The agent pointed to the left. "This way. I think we've made contact with someone trapped in the Tower. They're flashing a light in Morse code. We're trying to get some information from them, but there are problems."

"What problems?" Blancanales asked.

"Their Morse code is bad. Very slow, and they get some of the alphabet wrong. But they're getting across to us."

"Where are they?" Lyons asked.

"The fifty-third floor."

The agent in overalls opened an office suite's door. Lyons strode in. "Hey, Hardman Three! You missed the action!"

Gadgets said, "What action?"

Schwarz was in a stock broker's plush private office. Shipping blankets now covered the desk, the chairs, the bookshelves and the carpet. Consoles and recorder decks crowded the walls. At the window that overlooked the WorldFiCor Tower, tripods supported devices still in their vinyl cases. Gadgets stood at the window, looking out at the Tower through a pair of binoculars.

Twilight shadows and sunset glare broke the Tower's mirror walls into alternating patterns of black and fire. Here and there, lights showed in the other buildings on Wall Street. But very few lights broke the depthless black of the Tower's shadow patterns. One light blinked on and off, in dot–dash sequences.

"We interrupting anything?" Blancanales asked.

"Not really. Just a second." Gadgets kept the binoculars on the blinking light for another second, then went to an intercom phone. "You taking down the message? Great. I'm in conference."

Gadgets turned to them. "Hope their lives don't depend on their Morse. Because if they do, they're dead."

"What's happening in there?" asked Lyons, moving to the window.

"There's a man named Charlie Green on the fifty-third floor. There's a woman named Forde, I think, and some others. I sent their names downstairs. I don't know how they'll be able to help us. But—" Gadgets grinned "—I have got the most fas-ci-nating development. Remember what happened...wow, was it only last night? The big bang? It just about...."

"Wait!" Lyons interrupted. He looked at the liaison agent.

"I'll go," the agent offered.

"How about bringing up that fellow who wanted to talk to us?" Blancanales asked. "We can talk in the corridor out there. So that we don't compromise the mission. That okay with you?"

Lyons nodded. He waited until the liaison agent exited. "We can't say anything about Miami or North Carolina here. And the less any of these fellows know about what we do here, the better. Those are the instructions. What were you saying?"

"Like last night. The big bang? Listen." Gadgets went to a tape deck, rewound a few feet of tape, snapped the machine into forward. There was background hiss, then a blast of electronic noise.

"You mean a radio detonator?" Lyons asked. He looked to the Tower, stared.

"Yeah. I think it might even be the same one. Sounds the same."

"They tried to blow their people away? Again?"

"That is one organization I do not want to join," Gadgets joked.

"When was this?" Lyons demanded.

"When we were chasing around, trying to follow the Politician. I got back and I had it on tape. Either something went wrong inside the Tower, or the creeps in there weren't set up."

"Are there any negotiations?" Blancanales asked.

Gadgets laughed. "They want a ticker-tape parade."

"It's a set-up," Lyons spat out. "Those crazies in there were set up, the Tower was set up, and any negotiations are pointless. Whoever's running the action plans to blow the Tower away. And they've got their claws into WorldFiCor in ways we can't even imagine. Show our partner what we found."

"Take a look at this." Blancanales showed Schwarz the eight-by-ten. "We don't know who this one is. But guess who the other one is—the distinguished-looking guy? World Financial Corporation President E.M. Davis."

"Wow."

"We took these from a Vietnamese," Blancanales continued. "Maybe in a few hours we'll have the answers to about five hundred different questions, but until then we only have these photos."

The intercom phone buzzed. Gadgets took it.

"Who is this?"

"Taximan, sir. I'm downstairs in the Coordination Office. They've had a team watching Davis all day, as protective surveillance. In fact, they're following him around midtown Manhattan right now.''

"They're on Davis now.'' Gadgets gave Lyons the phone.

"What's he doing?'' Lyons demanded.

"Driving around talking to people. He's in the theater district.''

"How many cars and trucks does that surveillance team have?''

"Three, including us when we get there,'' said Taximan.

"You'll need more. And cars that he couldn't have seen during the day.''

"There's a lot of men out at the apartment, picking up pieces. Maybe when they . . . .''

"Maybe nothing! This could be critical. Put the equipment in the cab. Call the men at the apartment, have some of them join the surveillance team—''

"Just a second!'' Gadgets interrupted. "If all those cars are operating with FBI frequencies, the crazies could be monitoring them. Use the secure phones or don't chance it.''

"Yeah, that's right. But we only have those three secure phones. What about scramblers for the other cars?''

"Remember,'' Gadgets cautioned Lyons. "They used scramblers. They might just be prepared to unscramble FBI devices. Why don't you borrow my secure-phone. It's here somewhere.''

"Rosario, you want to put off that translation work for a while? This might be interesting,'' said Lyons.

"Might be more than interesting,'' agreed Blancanales.

Lyons spoke into the phone again. "Okay, Taxi. We got a plan in motion. And where's Smith, my chauffeur? We left him out at the apartment house, right?"

"He's back now. He didn't have a police escort, so...."

"Tell him to be ready to move. We're on our way downstairs." Lyons slammed down the phone.

Blancanales already had the secure phone in his hand, the photos of the go-between and Davis in his inside sports coat pocket. "Ready to go."

"If we can't get anything quick," Lyons told Gadgets, "we'll come back. Learn what you can from those people trapped in there. It could help a lot when we go in tonight."

"We're going inside tonight?"

"Can't wait till tomorrow! See you later!"

"*Adios*," Gadgets said. But his partners were already gone.

Lyons and Blancanales were running to the elevator when a voice called them back.

"Officers! Wait, please!"

The slight man Lyons had straight-armed a few minutes before was panting after them. He zipped open his folder. Inside, there was the badge of a United States Treasury Agent.

"So you're official," Lyons nodded. "I thought maybe you were a clerk from somewhere."

"Art Sands," the slight man told him, shaking hands with them both. "Actually, for the last four months, I *have* been a clerk. In WorldFiCor's Department of Data Systems. Mr. Brognola thought I should bring my information to you."

"Great. We're in a hurry."

"Listen. For several years, WorldFiCor, and several of its highest executive officers, have been the subject of an intensive investigation by the Internal Revenue Service. Because of the technological complexity of WorldFiCor's operations, the National Security Agency cooperated in the interception of the company's national and international transmissions of data. It was only after the IRS realized the scope of the frauds perpetrated that...."

"Quick, man," Lyons told him. "People could die while you're talking."

"Certainly. In short, there has been an embezzlement of WorldFiCor funds unprecedented in the history of finance. We believe...."

"Catch your own crooks! We don't have time for this." Lyons punched the elevator button again.

"Just a second," Blancanales cautioned. He turned to the Treasury Agent. "So how does this affect what's going on in the Tower?"

"We don't know," the man admitted. He handed Lyons and Blancanales each a collection of sheets covered with graphs and columns of numbers. "But a *billion dollars* is gone. And we don't have any idea where it went."

13

In the back of a customized van, Lyons checked the equipment. Outside, the reds and grays and golds of the sunset became the depthless turquoise of evening. Streetlights flickered on. In minutes it would be night. Through the tinted Plexiglass of the van's floor-to-roof side window, the headlights of a turning car flashed across the black metal of the M-16 that Lyons lifted from a phony trombone case.

"There any way we can block these side windows?" Lyons asked Smith, who sat alone in the front. "If somebody sees what I've got in here, the NYPD will drop a SWAT team on us."

"Pull down the shade, sir."

"Fancy." Lyons leaned to each of the two side windows, pulled down rolling shades.

"When they told me you asked for an M-16 with one of those night-sniper scopes, I knew we had to have this van," said Smith. "Couldn't have you trying to sight in on someone in that old Dodge I was driving."

"Thanks." Lyons pressed the lock on the M-16's actuator and hinged open the rifle. He flashed a penlight inside, saw gleaming, immaculate steel. It smelled of oil. He snapped the rifle shut, cocked it, pulled the trigger on the empty chamber. Then he tried to move the Starlite's mounts, but felt no wobble. He switched on the power, sighted out of one of the van's small back windows. Light standards, tree branches and distant windows flashed through his view. He slapped in an eighteen-round magazine, then returned the rifle to the trombone case.

The camera was more difficult. It was simply a 35 mm single-lens reflex camera with an electronic lens. An aluminum brace reinforced the assembly of the heavy lens and the camera, preventing the weight of the lens, electronics and battery from snapping the lens mount. An extension to the brace created a folding stock, like an assault rifle. For the left hand, there was a curved plastic grip. Lyons hit the power switch and sighted out the back windows.

"I think that thing would scare people worse than the M-16," Smith joked, watching Lyons in the rear-view mirror. "That thing looks like a space cannon."

"You know anything about cameras?" Lyons asked.

"Yes, sir. I graduated from the Academy. Photography is required."

"Then check this when you get the chance. It seems okay, but I wouldn't know."

"Yes, sir. We're coming up behind the surveillance cars now. Maybe you'd like to try those windows back there. They fold upward, so you can lie down on the carpet and put the rifle barrel out the side."

"What's the Bureau doing with a van like this?" Lyons joked, pushing up the folding window, then letting it fall down. He locked it closed. "It's perfect for direct action."

"You mean assassination?" Smith laughed. "It's

for providing emergency surprise-fire superiority in case a suspect gets heavy. Such as in a decoy operation. Problem is, it has to be parked sideways to the target.''

''That's no problem.'' Lyons checked the inside handle of the back door. It would unlock and swing open in an instant.

''Judging by what I've seen today,'' Smith said, turning and grinning at Lyons, ''it's the opposition that's got all the problems. Like staying alive.''

Lyons wasn't amused. ''Prone to overconfidence, are you? Now where's the cab? Where's the surveillance team?''

''The cab's two or three cars behind us. Surveillance team is right in front of us. Subject is stopped at the curb. Chauffeur is buying a newspaper. We're passing him. Look out your right window—there's the limo.''

A long black limousine slid through his view. Tinted side windows hid whoever might be a passenger. A chauffeur in a severe gray suit left a newsstand with a newspaper under his arm. Then the brilliant lights of a marquee and a neon window display lit the interior of the van. Lyons dropped the shade back. He keyed the secure phone. ''You see him?''

Blancanales answered immediately.

''No one could see him in that limousine.''

''Surveillance says he's still in there. Stay close for a few minutes. I'll have a conference with the team leader, give him a secure phone. The time's come to make something happen.'' Lyons returned the handset to the case and called forward to Smith, ''Pull up beside the team leader. I need to talk with him." He saw Smith pick up the microphone of the scrambler radio. "Don't use the radio! Pull up beside him."

"Sorry, sir. I didn't understand." Smith accelerated, weaving through traffic, and braked as he came even with an unmarked late-model Dodge.

Taking the extra secure phone, Lyons climbed from the van's back door, went around to the door of the Dodge.

"That's the man!" Smith called out. The two agents in the front seat turned and saw Lyons. One of them reached back, unlocked the back door. Lyons stepped in as the traffic light changed.

The agent in the passenger seat stared at Lyons. "So you're the hotshot. I'm Agent Tate. That's Agent Lopez. Your man in the van said you had a phone for us."

"A secure phone," Lyons told them, opening the case and passing it forward to them. They made no effort to take it from him. "Impossible to intercept or monitor. Hey, take it. It'll be your only connection to us."

"We don't need it," Tate told Lyons. "We got scramblers in our cars."

"Yeah, and maybe they do, too. Nothing concerning my partner and me, or what we do, is to be sent over the scramblers. We can't risk it."

"That's being a little paranoid, don't you think?" Lopez commented. He made a right turn. "Going back around to pick up the limo again."

"All day long I've been paranoid," said Lyons coolly. "It seems to be keeping me alive. And while we're on the subject of staying alive, why don't you paste an FBI insignia on each door of this car, make it official? A three-year-old could spot this Dodge. And your clothes—how about just wearing uniforms? What's the point of keeping Davis under surveillance if...."

"Hey, hotshot," Tate interrupted Lyons, "Mr. Davis is not a suspect in this case. What we're doing is called protective surveillance."

"That just changed. What we're going to do now is to help him make a break. He's out here to meet one of the crazies, and he won't do it while he's got agents watching him. So, you're going to lose him."

"What're you talking about?" Tate sneered. "That man is not a suspect. He is our responsibility. He is not to leave our sight. Those were our instructions. And we will follow them to the letter."

Lyons looked at the man for a long moment. "Do what I say or take a walk. Resign."

The scrambler buzzed. Lopez took the microphone. "Here."

A tinny, mechanical voice came from the speaker. "Do you have Davis in sight? He pulled away from us."

"No, we don't," Lopez replied. "We're circling to come up behind him again."

"You can't, because he's gone," the mechanical voice told them.

"Not a suspect?" Lyons asked. "Then why is he evading you?"

Tate snorted, reaching into the glove compartment. "He can't go anywhere. We got a D.F. on the limo."

"You don't have one on *him*." Lyons punched the secure phone. "Taxi! You on our man?"

"This is Taximan. Hardman Two saw Davis dodge into a theater crowd. He went after him."

Killing the connection, Lyons keyed the code for his own secure phone in the van. Smith answered immediately, "Your partner's in motion. What do you want me to do?"

"Hold on." Lyons put his hand over the mouthpiece. He leaned over the front seat, grinning at the agents. "Well, our distinguished gentleman just became a suspect. Do you fellows want to get with it?"

"No scramblers?" Lopez asked. "How do we contact the other car?"

"Use the scrambler with them," Lyons explained, "but don't mention us. We'll direct you with the secure phone. You follow the limo, make like nothing's changed. We'll follow him. If we need you, we'll call you on the secure phone."

"Davis isn't in league with those terrorists, is he?" Tate asked, his confidence shaken.

"I think they've got a hook in him," Lyons told him. "I'll brief you later." Lyons spoke into the secure phone. "Smith, pick me up."

Swinging open the sedan's door, Lyons jumped from the car. He ran a few steps through traffic and jumped to the curb. The unmarked sedan turned the corner, became one of the thousands of cars on Forty-second Street. Lyons watched the early evening diners and theater patrons walking past him. Some of the people, dressed in expensive fashions or conservative dinner clothes, saw him and veered away, keeping six feet of sidewalk between him and themselves.

He did look bad. He'd borrowed a sports jacket from the FBI's wardrobe of costumes. It didn't fit right, but there was no blood on it. Blood splatters stained his white shirt, however, and his tie was gone. He needed a shave. There was a puffy bruise over his left eye. And he needed a shower too.

Headlights swept by him. A door flew open. Lyons ran three steps, then leaped into the van's bucket seat. Smith whipped the wheel around, U-turned.

"Taxi's right behind Davis and your partner," Smith explained. "They're on Forty-second, but if we try to navigate that street, we'll lose time in traffic. I'm going to parallel them in the alley."

Smith swerved the van around an idling truck and jumped the curb. A young couple walking arm in arm on the sidewalk saw the van's headlights bearing down on them and ran screaming into the street. Smith whipped into the alley, accelerated. Lyons braced his hands against the dash as stairways, stage doors, trash bins, drunks flashed past at sixty miles an hour. Then Smith slammed on the brakes as they approached Sixth Avenue.

"You can look now," Smith said. "We're still alive."

"Look yourself," Lyons muttered out of the side of his mouth. "See that man in the gray suit? That's Davis."

Davis stood at the alley's curb, hesitating to cross in front of this apparently reckless van driver. Only after he was sure the van had come to a complete stop did he continue down the Avenue.

"And there's my partner." Lyons nodded at Blancanales. Hardman Two gave his partner a quick glance, motioned for Lyons to accompany him.

Lyons took a hand-radio and told Smith, "He wants me to come along. Every few minutes, I'll give you our location. Real quick. Don't call me unless you absolutely have to."

Joining the sidewalk crowd, Lyons hurried after the two men until he had both in sight. Then he cut through traffic to the other side of the Avenue, pacing Davis.

The sandy-haired man walked briskly, passing other pedestrians, hurrying through traffic lights, putting block after block behind him. From time to time, he stopped, apparently window shopping. But his eyes were not on the windows' merchandise, but on the reflections of the street, crowds, and traffic behind him.

They followed him almost eight blocks before he suddenly took a handful of coins from his pocket, got on a bus going back up to Forty-second Street. Both Lyons and Blancanales whipped out their hand-radios.

"I'm running after the bus," Lyons told Blancanales. "You get the cars in motion."

Without waiting for an answer, Lyons sprinted after the uptown bus. He ran on the opposite side of the avenue, dodging through groups of people to block Davis' view if he looked back. The bus driver accelerated from one stop to another up the one-way avenue, but he didn't race the lights. Lyons did.

At one intersection, the bus coasted through a yellow light. Lyons, half a block behind, sprinted until he came to the intersection, then slowed only long enough to glance at the traffic. He wove through the slow-moving cars, forced one or two to brake, then sprinted again. A city cop waved at him, blew his whistle, but didn't attempt pursuit.

Davis got off the bus at Forty-second Street and started walking over toward Times Square. Lyons slowed, keeping a hundred yards behind him, and spoke into his hand-radio.

"Forty-second Street West. Maybe going to Times Square."

Lyons saw the customized van pass him. Blancanales waved nonchalantly. Ahead of Lyons, Davis walked quickly through the crowds. A panhandler approached him. Davis shoved the man aside without a backward glance. He hurried to a passenger loading zone in front of a hotel, grabbed for a cab's door, but three men with suitcases blocked him and took the cab.

Davis scanned the pedestrians and street traffic. Lyons ducked into a doorway. He saw Davis step into traffic and wave down a cab.

"Hey. He's in a taxi. Don't lose him, he could go anywhere!"

In reply, Blancanales' laughter came through the hand-radio. "I think we'll be able to keep up. Get out on the curb, we'll pick you up. Bet Taximan had a heart attack when Davis waved him down!"

Less than a minute later, the van slowed in traffic. Lyons ran to the back door, jerked it open and jumped in. Blancanales passed him a bottle of mineral water. Lyons gulped it.

"You did those eight blocks in record time," Blancanales commented. He glanced at Smith. "Even the hot-rod here couldn't keep up."

"Where's the limo?" Lyons asked. "You think he could be doing this just to check for shadows?"

Blancanales keyed the secure phone, but Smith stopped him. "He's out of the taxi. Going into that hotel."

"Must be a thousand rooms in that place!" Blancanales exclaimed. "Pull up into the taxi zone. Maybe he's meeting someone in the lobby."

They peered through the hotel doors and watched Davis cross the lobby to the elevators. He punched the button and waited. When the doors opened, the indicator arrow pointed down.

"I'm going to the garage!" Lyons told them as he left the van.

He ran to the entrance of the hotel's underground garage. At the bottom of the ramp there was a glass-walled attendant's booth. The uniformed boy inside watched Lyons. Deep in the cavernous garage, another attendant parked a car, started back.

Davis left the elevator and called to the attendant. He gave the attendant a dollar and a set of keys. The attendant ran to fetch the car.

"Can I help you, sir?" The boy in the booth asked Lyons.

"No." Lyons turned around, returned to the sidewalk. He stood with his back against the plate glass of a hi-fi store and waited. Within seconds, Davis was driving up the ramp in a white Mercedes coupé. Lyons keyed his hand-radio.

"He took off, going north, in a white Mercedes sports model. I'm at the head of the ramp. Let's go!"

When the van reached him, Lyons got in the back and immediately checked the camera and light-intensifying lens. He switched on the lens power, glanced at the film-load indicator. Smith followed the Mercedes toward Central Park. Lyons aimed the lens through the van's side windows. He scanned the park's quiet darkness. He saw lovers on the lawns, late evening bicyclists, and a few kids. He saw it as if the night were day.

Focusing on a young girl riding a bicycle, he clicked off two frames to test the camera. Then he braced the lens between the front bucket seats and searched the traffic ahead for the Mercedes.

"Ready to go," Lyons told the other men. "Where's Taximan?"

"Up ahead of Davis. He said Davis tipped him a dollar...."

The Mercedes followed the curving drive through Central Park. It rejoined heavy traffic near the Dakota apartment building. Jaywalking tourists were slowing traffic somewhat. They saw Davis searching the sidewalks, looking for someone.

"This is it," Smith said. "Looks like he's looking for his man."

Lyons scanned the passersby with the lens. Hundreds of faces flashed through the viewfinder. Blancanales grabbed his shoulder and pointed.

"There, that guy. He saw the Mercedes. He's...."

Lyons caught a young man in the viewfinder. He followed the youth as he ran out to the Mercedes, snapping frame after frame. But it was when the young man paused at the side of the Mercedes, and put a lighter's flame to a cigarette that Lyons identified him.

Only the night before, in the North Carolina swamps, Lyons had seen that man light a cigarette as he unloaded high-powered explosives. Lyons now watched as the guy entered the Mercedes. Davis put an arm around the young man, hugged him. In the viewfinder, Lyons saw the two faces very clearly. The younger man had dark Latin skin; but his hair, remarkably, was sandy blond.

"They're hugging each other!" Smith said. "What are they, lovers?"

"No," Lyons corrected. "Father and son."

14

"It would be utterly beyond our authority!" Agent Tate's voice carried a touch of panic through the secure phone. "There'd be repercussions that you can't imagine. Mr. Davis is a personal friend of the President of the United States. And you're talking about grabbing him off the street like some kind of punk?"

"I don't care whose friend he is—" Lyons yelled down the phone at the agent. As he spoke he glanced through the windshield at the Mercedes, two cars ahead of the van. The van, the Mercedes, and the agent's taxicab moved among the hundreds of other cabs on the George Washington Bridge. The lights of New Jersey spread on the horizon ahead.

Inside the Mercedes, Davis and his son talked as they had for the previous several miles, Davis glancing to the young man, gesturing with one hand, the son waving his hands as he spoke, emphasizing his words with a clenched fist.

"—and I don't need to explain it to you. The President of the United States gave us the authority to break these crazies. And Davis is up in front of us talking business with one of them."

"What do you mean, talking business?" Tate asked him. "From what you've told me, you've got no proof the other man is a terrorist. Now you're asking...."

"Hey! Listen to me, Mr. Federal Agent. You were assigned to support my mission against the crazies. I asked you for assistance, and you have refused. This is it! Talk to you later."

Lyons hung up, leaned forward to Blancanales. "Tate told me Davis is a friend of the President. Said he wouldn't move against him. So we don't have any backup."

"You and me, huh?"

"What about me and Taximan?" Smith asked. "We got our instructions straight from Mr. Brognola. He told us to do what is necessary. So you can count on us."

"Yeah." Lyons smiled. He keyed the secure phone. "Taxi, you ready to help us take those two in the Mercedes?"

"Anytime. Give me the signal."

"Davis is a personal friend of the President. Right or wrong, there will be heavy, heavy flak."

"Like I said, give me the signal."

"There's one other man we're looking for, maybe they're on their way to talk to him. So hold on. Over."

"What's the plan?" Blancanales asked.

"We got two of them," Lyons said, thinking out loud. "But there's at least one more man, who might be back there in the city someplace. The go-between we saw in the photos. Or he might be inside the Tower. But I doubt it. I figure that anybody who's talked face to face with Davis wouldn't have been sent into the Tower. In case they were captured and interrogated."

"That makes sense," Blancanales agreed. "You think these two will meet up with him?"

"This little drive around town could just be a conference. If they meet the other man, we'll take all three. If not, we'll take Davis and his son before they split up. Chances are they're talking about the big bang problem."

They followed the Mercedes into New Jersey, turning off into quiet, modest residential neighborhoods. Davis made no effort to evade surveillance. They did not slow until they entered an industrial area.

Only one or two of the one-story corrugated metal factories had weekend night shifts. The parking lots of other factories and assembly plants were wastelands of asphalt and broken glass. The Mercedes turned from the boulevard, sped through a parking lot. At the far side of the lot, there was a line of parked semis and trailers. All but one of the trucks were blue and red with a merchandising company's insignia. The last truck was blue. It had no insignia.

When the Mercedes crossed the parking lot, the truck flashed its lights.

"This must be it."

Even as Lyons spoke, Smith whipped the van into an alley opposite the parking lot. The alley's darkness swallowed the van. Lyons keyed the secure phone.

"Taxi! Stay back! He's meeting...."

"I'm half a block back, with my lights off. Waiting for instructions."

Lyons put down the hand-set. Blancanales watched the parking lot in the van's side mirror.

"What're they doing?" Lyons asked.

"He's stopped the car. His son's getting out."

"You take the rifle, I'll put the camera on them." Lyons beamed the camera through the van's back window, got the Mercedes and semi in focus. Behind him, Blancanales took the M-16 from its case and chambered a round.

"Locked and loaded."

"The son's getting into the semi." Lyons watched as the young man went around the semi and climbed in on the passenger side. The electronics of the lens revealed another man behind the wheel of the truck.

"The go-between's in the truck," Lyons told the others. "Let's see what they do now."

Lyons clicked off a photo of the two men side by side in the cab of the truck. Then he zoomed back to include the Mercedes—with Davis waiting inside—in the photo. The lens brought out the features of the three men. Lyons clicked again.

The camera's electric motor advanced the film automatically. Lyons touched the focus. He wanted a perfect photo linking Davis to the other man.

As his fingertip came down on the shutter button, Lyons saw the son raise a pistol to the head of the go-between, and fire. Lyons snapped the photo at the same instant that the impact of the slug threw the man sideways, the bullet continuing through his head to shatter the tempered glass of the door's window, bits of sparkling glass raining like diamonds onto the Mercedes.

"The crazy just put a bullet through the driver's head." Lyons' voice was calm, slow. "I've got a picture of it. With Davis in it."

"Jesus!" Blancanales' usual calm had snapped.

"Wait till you see it. We have a real-for-live court case against them. I think I'll even read them their rights." Lyons keyed the secure phone. "Move it, Taxi. He just killed a man. Be careful, play it by ear. We don't have any backup."

As soon as Lyons spoke to the cabbie, Smith slammed the van into reverse. It shot backwards from its hiding place behind a factory wall, and continued across the boulevard, Smith whipping the wheel around, accelerating and burning rubber. The taxi was only an instant behind them.

Both cars hurtled toward the Mercedes and truck. The young man was half out of the truck's cab when he saw the van and the taxi speeding toward them. He reached into his jacket pocket for his pistol.

Blancanales raised the M-16.

"Don't kill him!" Lyons shouted. "Smith, sideways!" But Smith had anticipated the command, was veering to the side, giving Blancanales a clear line of fire through the open side window. His shot hit the young man in the foot, slamming him against the truck. Then he fell backward to the asphalt.

Davis gaped at his son falling, and lost his chance to escape as the cab screeched to a stop in front of the Mercedes and Taximan leaped out, his pistol pointed at Davis' face. The older man raised his hands. A second later, Lyons and Blancanales jumped from the van, pointing pistols down at the stunned young man.

The .223 had torn away the heel of his fashionable shoe. He held his foot in both hands, rolling on the asphalt, his face twisted in pain.

"Good shot." Lyons grinned at Blancanales. Then

he took a card from his wallet, chanted aloud: "You are under arrest. You have the right to remain silent. You may...."

New York's columns of lights wheeled around them as the helicopter banked. Lyons saw the helipad's rectangle of red landing lights in the window in defiance of gravity. Then the lights sank and the sawtooth horizon of skyscrapers and night returned. The helicopter dropped straight down for landing. Lyons continued the interrogation of Davis and his son, whose Colombian driver's license identified him as Roberto Alcantara.

"We have photos of you together." Lyons told them. "We have photos of you—" he pointed at Alcantara "—with the pistol in your hand as you killed that man. The New York courts can send you away for life. But if you cooperate, we will not surrender you to North Carolina, where you killed two people last night. In that state, murder and conspiracy to commit murder are punishable by death. Do you understand? You have the choice between life or death."

Davis sneered, his gray aristocratic face becoming ugly, cunning. "We would like to speak to my lawyers immediately, if you don't mind. And there are several calls I'd like to make."

The helicopter bumped down. Agents on the roof threw the side doors open. Lyons grinned at Davis. "Oh, but I do mind."

Agents jerked the handcuffed Davis from his seat, quick-marched him across the roof to an open door. Lyons turned to Alcantara.

"You get special, extra-special personal attention." Lyons shoved Alcantara from the helicopter. Blancanales followed one step behind them. Agents half-dragged the limping Alcantara to the doorway and hustled him to the elevator. Before the doors closed, Lyons looked into the cold, sneering face of Alcantara. The man's face was a replica of his father's: younger, darker, but his hair certainly the same, and with the same ice-blue eyes, the same expression.

"If you want to live," Lyons told him, "you will cooperate with us."

"My father's lawyers will speak to you of this entirely unjustified arrest. You will soon learn that there are some men the police cannot touch."

Lyons grinned, looked at Blancanales. "Who said we're police?"

He saw Alcantara's sneer fail for an instant.

Speaking through an electronically secured telephone line to Washington, D.C., Lyons briefed his commander. "His son's name is Roberto Alcantara. The mother met Davis when he was working in Colombia twenty-five years ago. There was no room in Davis' career for a scandal and divorce, so he bought the woman off. Then he paid for the best schools, the best university for the boy. Along the way, Alcantara picked up some very red political ideas. He only saw eye to eye with his father when they decided to put their heads together and buy a country."

"Buy?" said Brognola.

"Yeah. Seems so. Either buy one, or buy into one. It apparently irritated Davis that his son couldn't inherit WorldFiCor. So they worked out a scheme. Alcantara got the weapons and explosives, recruited the crazies. Davis got the money to pay for it all through a variety of international embezzlements, the latest involving a disgruntled Hungarian ex-Communist. Davis would have been the king, and his son the prince. But judging from how Alcantara operates, Davis would have died fast, and Alcantara would have been the number one man.''

"This is great background,'' Brognola told him. "But listen now—how is this information going to get the terrorists out of the Tower?''

"There's more,'' Lyons said. "First of all, there's no way we can get in from the ground. Period. They have this psycho named Zuniga who spent months preparing for this. The garage and first floor are crisscrossed with booby-traps. No bomb squad or anti-terrorist team could get through in less than a day or two. Second, the Tower is wired with explosives and incendiaries. Alcantara intended to blow away the Tower with his crazies inside. That would have eliminated both the crazies and the WorldFiCor records.

"But something went wrong. Alcantara pushed the button and nothing happened.

"If Zuniga doesn't know the radio-detonator has failed, great. No problem. But if he does, there's no way he'll leave the Tower without a way to detonate the charges. Could be a fuse, a timer, something improvised. One wrong step and it's all over.

"Third, we're up against complete psychos. They won't be taken prisoner. When we rush them, if we give them time to think, they'll blow the whole show away. No doubt about it. So those are the three strikes against us.''

"You're saying we can't break them?'' Brognola asked.

"Not me. I'm just telling you what we're up against. On the positive side, the crazies have set their evacuation in motion. You heard that they finally asked for a helicopter?''

"Right. Three minutes ago.''

"Alcantara had told them to demand a helicopter to take them from the Tower helipad to a secret location upstate. Then he'd get them out of the country. Of course, that was all make-believe. Alcantara intended them to be blown sky high. But because that didn't happen, they've followed orders and demanded the chopper.''

"So how does the helicopter figure in your plans? You want to be in it when we send it, come down on the terrorists? That's exactly what they'll expect.''

"No, I've got a trick they won't expect. One of those crazies in the Tower, Zuniga, knows who their leader is. He's the only one who's seen and talked with Alcantara. I want two helicopters in the air, one from the City of New York to take the terrorists away, as negotiated, and the second a big tourist chopper, with Alcantara on it. He'll come down, go straight to Zuniga, tell him it's a last-minute change of plan to confuse the feds. And in the time it takes to explain the change to Zuniga and the other psychos, we'll come up behind them and put them down. It's the only way I can figure to create confusion.

"And we can get Alcantara to do it. He's a complete coward. It's one thing for him to tell his crazies to terrorize and murder and maim people, but when we put a blow-torch up near his face, he told us everything. That poor little rich boy will do anything we tell him.''

"And how does that defuse the bomb down below?"

"I'll have Alcantara ask Zuniga for the trigger unit to radio-detonate the building—so he can have the honor, et cetera. If Zuniga gives it to him, great. If not, Alcantara will ask for an explanation. We'll have Alcantara wired for sound, of course. As soon as Zuniga tells him how the charges are fused, we hit them. Then we defuse the charges."

"You said when they go up on the roof, you'll come up behind them. How will you get into the Tower?"

"That's the easiest part. There's some people trapped on the fifty-third floor. Zuniga's crew doesn't know they're up there—yet. We'll shoot a cable through the window, slide in."

"I don't like it, Lyons. You'll be taking some long chances."

"Sir, the crazies want the helicopter there in fifty-five minutes. They said they'll kill a hostage for every minute of delay. Quite simply, I can't come up with a better plan. It's the only chance they have, those thirty or forty people in there. . . .''

15

Working slowly because of their improvised tools, Charlie Green and two of his office staff, Jill and Diane, carefully removed the screws fastening the window's molding to the steel window frame. In the outer office and corridor, Sandy and Mrs. Forde stood guard. The Federal Agents in the building opposite the Tower had code-signaled Green and his staff to dismantle this particuliar window and remove the plate glass. The agents had emphasized in repeated Morse that the lives of everyone in the building depended on the window not falling to the sidewalk. If it did, the terrorists would be alerted.

"Done up here," Green told the others. He dropped the last screw, left the molding in place, let his arms fall to his side. Standing on a desk, he'd had his arms above his head for thirty minutes. His arms ached.

"I'm going as fast as I can," Diane told him.

"Me, too," Jill added.

"How many more?" Green asked. He saw blood dripping from Diane's hands. "Take a break, Diane."

"Damn it, my blister's popped."

"Go check on Mrs. Forde and Sandy, tell them we're almost ready to take out this window."

"Done down here," Jill told him. "Look! They're flashing the code again."

Across the street, the agents signaled again. Green interpreted the blinking light. "They want us to hurry."

"Are you going to answer them?"

"I'm going to pull out this window is what I'm going to do." Green dropped the last screw from the side molding, jammed the screwdriver between the aluminum molding and the steel frame, and levered carefully. Gooey plastic caulking stretched. Green got his fingers around the molding and pulled with all his strength. The molding slowly tore away from the plastic. He threw down that strip, went to the others. Finally, he ripped away the last molding strip.

Only plastic caulking held the eight-by-six-foot sheet of plate glass in the frame. Green tried to lever out the plate glass with a screwdriver. The glass chipped. He tried to pull it out with his fingertips. Blood ran from his shaved fingers.

"What's wrong, Mr. Green?" Jill asked.

"The window's glued in there with plastic!" Across the gulf between the two buildings, Green saw the federal agents' code-light blinking incessantly.

Five minutes, the code repeated. Five minutes. Five minutes.

He scraped the plastic away from the glass, cleared a foot of plastic in thirty seconds. *One foot in thirty seconds*, he thought. He looked at the sheet of glass. *And I've got twenty-eight feet of window edge to do.*

Then he looked through the edge of the glass. Plastic caulking cemented the other side, too! Even if he scraped away all the interior plastic, the exterior caulking would still hold the window in place.

"Find a cigarette lighter, matches!" he shouted to Jill. "Right now! Hurry!"

They tore through the drawers of the office. Whoever used this particular office wasn't a smoker. They went into another office, finally found a book of matches.

When they returned to the window, the light across the street flashed four. Four.

Green put a flame to the plastic. It softened, then burned. A line of flame ran up the window's edge. He soon had all the caulking in flames. The plate glass made cracking sounds as the burning plastic heated it. He saw burning plastic flow down the outside of the window.

Jamming his screwdriver into the frame again, Green levered. Flames burned his hands. But the glass moved.

In the corridor, pistol shots!

Black-suited for battle, Lyons paced the office. He checked the straps of his nylon harness for the tenth time. The steel mountaineering hook clanged against the silenced CAR-16 slung over his shoulder. He smoothed the Velcro flaps of the pockets holding the spare magazine for the CAR. He touched the pouches of concussion grenades.

At the office window, Blancanales waited with a high-powered compound bow. He had an arrow ready in place. A fishing reel attached to the bow held three hundred feet of monofilament. At his side was a coil of nylon rope. One end of the rope was already knotted around a steel beam above the office's acoustic-tile ceiling.

Federal agents clustered near the window. One held a flashlight with a long tube extension pointed at the window across the street. He urgently repeated the Morse code message. Another agent watched the window through binoculars.

"What goes on with those people?" Lyons shouted.

The agent with the binoculars turned to him. "They've got some kind of problem with the window."

"Look!" Blancanales pointed. It was then that they saw the window framed in flame.

Taximan, still wearing his cab-driver's uniform, arrived in the crowded office. "The helicopters are circling at two miles out, waiting for your signal."

Then Gadgets came through the door. He pushed past Taximan. Like Lyons and Blancanales, he wore battle-black and had a silenced CAR-16 slung over his shoulder. In each hand he carried several small electronic devices. "Last-minute trick. Here, radio in the front pocket, here's the earphone."

"More walkie-talkies?" Lyons asked. "I've got two already."

"These pick up their frequency. See the knob?" Gadgets explained as he slipped the small radio into Lyons' pocket. "We can monitor them. But when things get moving, twist the knob. It'll jam their walkie-talkies."

"Any chance they'll be monitoring us?"

"I don't think so. The truck out in New Jersey had all their serious electronics in it." Gadgets looked over at the flaming window. "What's going on over there?"

They saw the plate-glass window drop back into the office. A young woman waved her arms. Blancanales raised the bow, drew back, but didn't let the arrow fly.

"Go!" Lyons told him. "Make your shot!"

"Signal for her to get out of the way," Blancanales told the agent with the flashlight.

"We got three minutes! Make your shot!"

The arrow arced through the night, monofilament singing from the reel.

Shivering in the chill wind, Mrs. Forde explained what had happened. "Diane came out of the office and told me we were almost ready for the officers to come in. Sandy wasn't paying attention to the elevators, she wanted to hear what we were saying.... Then the two creeps with guns came out of the elevator. She didn't see them until I shot at them.

"I think I hit one. But they grabbed Sandy, took her with them." She was almost hysterical.

"Did you watch what floor they went to?" Green asked her.

"The third floor. They went straight down to the third floor."

"Okay, calm down. Get out of the wind. The shakes will go away, don't worry." Green pried the pistol out of Mrs. Forde's hands, checked the cylinder. He pulled out two brass casings. "Reload your pistol. They could come back."

Jill was standing in broken plate glass, hauling in monofilament, hand over hand. In seconds, they had a heavy nylon rope in their hands. Green stood on the desk, ripped a hole in the false ceiling, looped the rope over a steel beam. He pulled the rope taut, knotted it. Then he hung by his hands from the rope to test the knot. The nylon was as tight as an iron rod.

The nylon line angled up to the building across the street, three floors higher. Green waved his arms. He saw the signal flash in response.

A shadow stepped from the far window, and started to hurtle towards Green. He stared for an instant at the man in black sliding through space. Then he remembered his own training and experience, years before. He quickly checked the office for obstacles. The desk!

Green shoved the desk aside, kicked away a chair. The blond, wide-shouldered man in a commando's black jumpsuit flew through the window, jerked to a halt, dropped to the floor in a crouch.

"Officer!" Green called out. "They know we're here. The terrorists...."

The man in black glanced at Green with cold blue eyes, stepped past him, flashed a light to the opposite building. In twenty-five seconds, two more men in black were in the small office. Then the blue-eyed commando turned again to Green.

"They may know you're here," he told Green, "but they're too busy to come back. Take your people to another floor now. Hide. It'll all be over in ten minutes. Whatever you do, don't go down to the ground floor. Understand?"

"They took one of my staff with them!"

But the three men in black were already gone. Green ran after them. He saw the elevator doors slide shut. The indicator light went to the ninety-seventh floor, and stopped. Then it continued to the hundredth floor.

"I thought they were going to rescue us!" Jill cried.

"What now?" Mrs. Forde asked.

"You and the other two take the stairs down to the next floor," Green told her. "Lock yourselves in an office and wait. They said it will be over in a few minutes. It looks like there's going to be shooting. Don't leave the office once you're in there."

"What about you?" asked Diane.

"They took Sandy, and she's my responsibility." Green strode to the elevator and punched the down button.

As he dropped to the fifth floor, he took the .45 pistol from his coveralls pocket and slipped the safety.

From the ninety-seventh floor, the Able Team took the stairs. Lyons went first. He moved as fast as he dared through the stairwell's half-darkness, peering around corners, waving his flashlight across the landings to check for booby traps. His caution cost precious seconds.

He whispered into his radio's mike. "Team moving to Position Two, over."

In his right ear, he heard the response from the command center: "Check, over." In his left ear, through the radio monitoring the terrorists' frequency, he heard only an occasional word or phrase in Spanish, too colloquial and quick for him to understand. He pulled the earphone out of his ear and tucked it into his pocket.

The concrete shaft of the stairwell echoed with sounds from far below them. There was a voice, a clank of metal on metal. Lyons glanced back to Blancanales and Gadgets. They moved quickly, silently, as if they were shadows without flesh. The distant sounds continued.

At the landing of the hundredth floor, one flight of stairs short of the stairwell housing that opened to the roof, Lyons unscrewed the 40-watt light bulb. He called Blancanales forward. They talked in the dark, their CAR-16's aimed at the roof door.

"What are you hearing on the monitor?" Lyons asked. "I can't make out the Spanish."

"They're behind us. The shooting on the fifty-third floor slowed them down. We got an extra two minutes. What about the door? Any way we can check it?"

"I'll chance it. Alcantara said the plan was for the lower floors only to be wired. So back off, I'm going up. And kill that light down there; someone could be waiting for me when I go out that door."

Blancanales touched Lyons' shoulder. "*Adios.*"

Lyons laughed. "Don't get sentimental." When Blancanales blacked out the landing and had taken cover, Lyons crept to the roof door. He ran his hand along the steel door frame, felt nothing. Then he flattened himself against the wall, and started to ease the door open.

The cool evening wind touched his face. He heard the distant throbbing of the helicopters. Lyons didn't continue through the door. It made no sense to him that the door wasn't booby-trapped. Unless this was the way the crazies intended to take to the helipad.

Even if that's true, he thought, they should have it set so we can't follow them.

He couldn't risk a flashlight. Instead, he took a slip of paper from his pocket, a diagram of the WorldFiCor rooftop area, and tore off a strip. Using it like a feeler, he ran it along the doorframe.

Just above ankle height, the paper caught on something. Lyons touched it again, then laid himself down on the landing and looked closely.

There, finer than a hair, glinting with starlight, a transparent strand of filament extended from one side of the doorway to the other. Lyons checked for other trigger-strands. Then he spoke into the radiomike.

"We got one here. One line of filament, ankle high. I'm going on."

Carefully he stepped over it. He found the charge: it was a kilo of C-4. Then he continued, scanning the rooftop and helipad for terrorists. He lifted his feet high as he walked. He couldn't search the entire roof for booby traps, but he would have to do all he could to avoid the trip-lines.

Making it to the elevator's motor housing opposite the helipad, he felt carefully again for trip-lines or pressure triggers, then went up the ladder. On top, he spoke into his mike.

"Hardman One in position. Next, please. And good luck."

Blancanales came out, took his position in the air-conditioning stacks across the helipad from Lyons. Finally, Gadgets took a position on top of the stairwell housing. Regardless of how the terrorists came out—elevator or stairs—the Able Team had them in triangular ambush.

"Hey," whispered Gadgets suddenly. "They're on their way! Oh, good God! Politician, did I hear that Spanish right? Tell me I didn't."

"You did," Blancanales answered, his voice infinitely weary and sad. "All right, that's it. Let's do the best we can to save the hostages that the psychos bring up here. Zuniga has just poured gasoline on the ones he left downstairs. There's nothing we can do for them now."

16

It was happening in the auditorium on the mezzanine floor.

"You filthy Yankee scum!" Zuniga ranted from the auditorium's stage. "I will cleanse the earth of you. I will give you a few minutes of hell before Satan takes your souls for his inferno!"

Behind their packing-tape gags, the prisoners' faces contorted in silent screams, their eyes wide.

"You will die in flames for the sins of your Empire! There! Look there!" Zuniga pointed to the projection port at the back of the auditorium. On his cue, Ana smashed out the glass. She placed a box at the edge of the port. "You die when that bomb explodes! May your souls burn forever!"

Zuniga laughed. As he left the stage, he glanced at some prisoners who did not seem to be in a panic. Three of the young executives—two men and a woman—had already freed their hands and feet. They didn't scream or struggle. They waited for their chance to escape. They would be the leading players in Zuniga's comedy.

In the corridor, the members of his squad shoved and kicked several hostages into groups of two, then knotted nylon line around the prisoners' throats. Each squad member had two hostages who would

serve as human shields when they stepped out onto
the Tower's roof. The squad would take some into
the helicopter, leave the others to die when the Tower
exploded. The hostages in the helicopter would live
only a few minutes more.

Zuniga blocked the auditorium doors and set the
charges. The prisoners inside would break down the
doors quickly, detonating the charges, which in turn
would detonate the ton of C-4 and incendiaries.

"Fernando!" Zuniga called out.

"Yes, commander!"

"You remain here. Scream at them. Rave. When
the helicopter is ready, I will signal. Then you come
up to the roof. Understand?"

"I will come when you signal."

Each with a pair of hostages, the squad waited.
Rico had the young blonde woman they had captured
only minutes before on the fifty-third floor. He
twisted the rope savagely around her throat. He
kicked her into the elevator, and jerked her to her
feet when she fell.

"Careful, *compadre*," Zuniga warned. He
glanced at his watch. "She must live another two
minutes."

Zuniga pressed the elevator button marked RH for
roof/helipad.

Lyons felt the cables and motors start to vibrate in
the elevator's housing beneath him. He spoke into his
throat-mike: "Here they come. Helicopter, come on
down. Any problems with our guest star?"

"He is one very frightened man."

"They just came out the door! Over."

Turning up the volume on Alcantara's body-mikes, Lyons heard the man's petulant voice complaining over the noise of the rotors. "... the vileness of your threats.... I thought this was a civilized country.... I don't believe you'd dare...." Lyons flicked off the safety on his CAR-16.

Have no doubts, Mr. Alcantara, Lyons said to himself. *We have the nerve, all right.*

Clutching a hostage against him and holding his M-16 at ready, Zuniga left the elevator, stepped over the filament and into the rotor storm. He scanned the rooftop for ambushers, saw no one. He motioned for his squad to follow, cautioning each one about the booby trap, then shoved his first hostage ahead of him and dragged the second behind him. She staggered, fell, choked as Zuniga pulled her to her feet by the rope around her neck.

He heard the second helicopter and looked up. He warily approached the helicopter on the pad. He pointed his automatic rifle through the side-door.

"Is this a trap, *federales*? If it is, you all die!"

Alcantara, his leader through all the months of planning and preparation—who had given Zuniga's pointless life meaning, who had brought his lifetime of hatred to flower—stepped from the helicopter. The landing lights made his coward's face seem like a mask of blood.

"Zuniga! My compatriot! Yes, they planned a trap for you! But I learned of it and changed the plans.

The helicopter will take us all to freedom! *Victory is ours!"*

Too surprised to speak, Zuniga said nothing. His leader, who had always been so proud and aloof, aristocratic, strangely blond, threw his arms around Zuniga, embraced him.

"Where is the detonator, my friend?" Alcantara asked him, his voice almost begging. "May I have the honor of pushing the button?"

Lifting the walkie-talkie to his lips, Zuniga called down to Fernando. "We are ready, come now. *Viva Puerto Rico libre!"*

Zuniga turned to his leader, studied his face. Alcantara's smile quivered, became a grimace of fear. Now Zuniga knew.

"How could you have learned what the *federales* intended?" And he raised his M-16 to Alcantara's throat. The burst ripped away his leader's head.

From the third-floor stairwell, Charlie Green heard the psycho screaming curses in Spanish. He inched the door open, saw a young Puerto Rican in a moving company's overalls pacing the corridor, turning every few seconds to laugh or shout at the closed doors of the company auditorium. The doors' handles were lashed together.

Across the corridor, near the elevators, Green saw stacked army-drab crates.

Through the inch-wide space, Green watched, waiting for his chance. He held the .45 pistol pointed straight up, the hammer at full cock, safety off. His sweat made the grip clammy. Sweat trickled down his arm. If the terrorist had put Sandy in the auditorium, he'd free her and any other people the terrorists might have taken prisoner. He would tell them about the commando team upstairs. If Sandy wasn't there, he'd take the psycho's M-16 and go find her. He liked Sandy. She had introduced her husband to him at a company party: they were a beautiful young couple with a two-year-old child. It was Green who had called her to work that morning. She was his responsibility. Period.

The psycho's walkie-talkie buzzed. A few words blared from the speaker, then he slung his rifle over his shoulder, went to the elevator, pushed the "up" button. Green knew it would take the terrorist two seconds to unsling his rifle, chamber a round and fire.

Sprinting, his running shoes silent on the corridor carpeting, Green crossed the twenty yards separating them before the young man could jerk the rifle from his shoulder. The .45 was less than a foot from the terrorist's face when Green fired. The slug entered the psycho's gaping mouth, tore his head from his lower jaw, spraying brains and blood and bone over the immaculate chrome of the elevator doors.

Pulling the rifle from the twitching corpse, Green chambered a round, flipped the lever to full auto, and watched the elevator doors. The car came, the doors sliding open to reveal the empty interior.

He turned to the auditorium. Someone on the other side pushed against the doors. Green heard a voice inside: "Is he still there?"

"No," Green answered. "He's dead."

"Who's that?" The voice called through the doors.

"Charlie Green, Eastern European Accounts. Is Sandy Robinson in there?"

"Get us out of here!" voices screamed. "There's a bomb in here!"

Green tore at the ropes binding the door handles.

When they saw the muzzle-flash of the terrorist's M-16 on the helipad below them, the federal agents circling in the second helicopter hit the switch powering the Xenon searchlight. Ten thousand watts of white light created a disorienting noon on the roof-top.

An agent in the helicopter recorded the slaughter on high-resolution video tape for later analysis. It only lasted seconds.

But for Lyons and his partners Blancanales and Schwarz, the few seconds were hours.

From their positions around the helipad, they looked into the confused group of terrorists and hostages, crowded shoulder to shoulder, their heads only inches apart.

Lyons had anticipated this. Before entering the Tower, he had requested, and received, specially loaded 5.56mm cartridges for their CAR-16's. The standard 50-grain military and the 55-grain hollow-point hunting slugs used with the 5.56mm cartridge had a maximum kill range of four hundred yards. At close range, regardless of the slug used, the 2700-feet-per-second muzzle velocity of the CAR's would create through-and-through wounds, the slug continuing through the body of the target to perhaps kill or maim someone beyond. Knowing that the combat would be at close range, with the terrorists shielding themselves behind hostages, Lyons had Able Team's weapons loaded with specially cast hollow-point slugs.

The 40-grain bullets were actually lead cups, their interior voids packed with common lubricating wax to give the slug additional weight. These slugs, though unstable and inaccurate at distances exceeding one hundred feet, had the advantage of dissipating the bullet's striking energy of 1200 foot/pounds within inches of the point of penetration.

Impact opened the cup from its diameter of 5.56mm to a disc of approximately 25mm, resulting in the instantaneous dissipation of the striking energy and the conversion of the lubricating wax filler into expanding gas.

At the sound of Zuniga's auto-burst, Lyons and Blancanales and Gadgets became mechanical marksmen. To them their work appeared in slow motion.

The first radical hollow-point from Lyons' CAR-16 struck Zuniga just above his right ear. His head ceased to exist, only the blood-spurting stump of his neck and a few ragged strips of jaw and scalp remaining. The impact threw the corpse and the two hostages to the helipad asphalt.

Simultaneously, slugs from Blancanales' and Gadgets' rifles killed Rico and Julio. Staring up at the second helicopter, Rico had turned to ask instructions of his squad leader, his jaw moving to form the first word of the question. Blancanales' slug hit him at the base of his skull. The jaw and brains and pink fragments of skull struck Ana in the face and chest.

Julio had been startled by the sound of Zuniga's burst, was straightening suddenly. Gadgets' bullet hit him just above the collar-bone, slamming his head back as his throat and spine exploded. His head flopped forward, attached to his torso by only a few ligaments and strips of skin, as his corpse fell.

Brains and blood on her face, Ana's eyes went wide at the sight of a jaw falling onto her chest, the teeth brilliantly white in the Xenon light. A scream rising in her throat was never heard, the breath from her contracting lungs hissing through the gore and torn tissue of a throat without a head, spraying blood-mist into the Xenon glare. Lyons' second target fell, the rope binding her hostages falling from her spasming hands.

Lyons sighted on Luisa, touched the trigger as Blancanales' second shot snapped her head forward. Lyons' bullet entered the woman's exploding skull, destroyed her again.

But Carlos ducked, pulled his shields—a man and a woman—backwards as he scrambled for safety. One-handed, he jerked his rifle up. The female hostage courageously, instinctively blocked the rifle with her elbow, pushing the barrel down. The magazine emptied into the asphalt.

Three slugs caught Carlos simultaneously. Each member of Able Team sighted on whatever part of the terrorist's body was visible from his particular angle. Lyons' shot snapped his spine, dumped the terrorist's guts from his body. Blancanales' shot tore away the terrorist's entire face. Gadgets annihilated his left leg.

"*Cease fire!*" Lyons shouted.

Bodies covered the helipad. Some moved, some twitched with the impulses of dying nerves. Able Team scanned the carnage for anyone with a rifle still alive. Hostages twisted away from the corpses. Men and women sobbed. Someone laughed.

The man whom Carlos had held as a shield struggled to his feet and looked down at the disintegrated terrorist in horror. "There's one more downstairs!" he managed. "One of them's still down below!"

Lyons leaped from his position. He saw Blancanales climbing down from the air-conditioning stacks, and ran to him.

"Why did Zuniga kill Alcantara?"

"Alcantara said he learned of a trap," said Blancanales, "that he'd changed the plans. Zuniga asked him how he could have known of a trap, and pulled the trigger on him. But I think it was the way Alcantara was acting—Zuniga saw something was wrong."

"What did he say about the detonator?"

"Nothing. He called down to someone else, said they were ready now. And said '*Viva Puerto Rico Libre.*' Then he shot Alcantara."

"A suicide man? To trigger the bomb?"

Blancanales changed magazines on his CAR-16. "Let's go find out."

Gadgets ran from the stairwell housing. "I've killed this booby trap," he said, "at least across the stairhead."

"Okay. Now watch the elevator after we go down," commanded Lyons. "The last guy could slip past us somehow."

A tall, middle-aged woman in a blood-splashed pants suit called out to them. "They're all in the auditorium, second floor. There's still time to save them."

Lyons and Blancanales ran to the elevator.

Tearing away the first loop of nylon cord holding the auditorium doors closed, Green shouted to the hysterical employees inside.

"Back off! Just a second! I can't untie the ropes with you pushing."

"Cut them! Please, get us out of here!"

"I don't have a knife. I can't go looking—just a second!"

He glanced around the corridor. He saw the stacked boxes, a few discarded lengths of nylon rope, a woman's shoe, a black nylon bag. But no knives, no bottles to break, nothing. He started over to the dead terrorist lying near the elevator doors.

Green stopped. For the first time in the sixty seconds since he'd killed Fernando, he stood still. He read the wording on the crates stacked against the elevator column.

"United States Army" had been marked over with stenciled letters. He didn't immediately recognize the stenciled letters. The lettering and words were Vietnamese!

On the end of one crate, he saw the letter and number: C-4.

A twisted plastic rope ran from the boxes. Green was standing on the rope. He looked down at his feet, then to the rope behind him. It extended from the U.S. Army packing crates to the discarded nylon bag. The bag had been thrown into the corner near the auditorium doors.

A strip of tape secured the bag's strap to the wall. Green saw a gossamer strand of monofilament stretched from the bag, across the auditorium's double doors, to the other side of the doors. A second strip of tape, only an inch long, secured the monofilament to the wall.

Green's heart stopped. He stood on a line of detonation cord. He recognized it from Vietnam. The det-cord ran from the stacked crates to the nylon bag. A line of monofilament stretched across the doors from the bag.

The panicked people in the auditorium threw their weight against the doors, pulling the nylon cord taut. The doors opened half an inch, fell closed again. Once more, the people threw their bodies against the doors.

One of the door handles broke. The door opened a half inch. Green saw the opening doors press against the monofilament.

His body moved so slowly. His brain screamed words, but his throat and tongue and lips didn't have the time to form the sounds. He threw himself at the doors, fell. He hit the doors with his back, pushed against the weight of the people hitting the doors.

He tried to scream the words again. This time he succeeded in mouthing the sounds.

"There's a bomb on the door!"

But they hit the doors again and again. Suddenly, two of the officers in black commando suits appeared, ran to him. The blond man threw himself against the doors.

Green and the officer stood side by side, pushing back the doors. The other officer—the bullnecked Latin man with gray in his black hair—traced the line of monofilament, peeling the tape off the far wall, letting the line go slack.

The officer went to the center of the corridor and whipped a knife from his boot to cut the det-cord. He threw the ends of the det-cord apart. Then he went to the black nylon bag, and very, very carefully cut the det-cord where it emerged from the bag.

The doors burst open and a wide-eyed mob of people poured into the corridor, some of them continuing to run in all directions as if from a fire.

"There's another bomb in there!" yelled a middle-aged woman. "Up in the projection room."

The blond officer disappeared into the cavern of the now-empty auditorium, as his partner attempted to control the disorder of the escapees with instructions for their calm descent to the ground floor.

Within a minute, he returned with the bomb. As he came by the alarmed Charlie Green, he said, "It's a fake. Just a transistor radio."

"Oh, man, what a relief," gasped Charlie.

"Mr. Green, you deserve a medal," said Carl Lyons.

Green laughed. "I already have medals. All I want to do is find a missing employee and then go home. I really wish I hadn't come to work today."

"We're glad you did," shouted Blancanales above the babble of the three dozen overjoyed people milling about him. "It's good to have the asssistance of a concerned citizen."

Blancanales disentangled himself from the men

and women lining themselves up to go downstairs.

"Now we must rescue Gadgets from that mess on the roof," he suggested to Lyons, who was inspecting the crates of C-4, "and let the three of us get the hell out of here. The cops can clean up the garage—it'll take them a week at least."

Mr. Green had disappeared in search of Sandy Robinson, and a pall of silence descended on the floor.

"You have never spoken truer words," murmured Lyons. "This building stinks. Let's get out of here."

ABLE TEAM

AN EXECUTIONER SERIES

#2 The Hostaged Island
ON SALE MAY!

Able Team—Carl Lyons, Pol Blancanales and Gadgets Schwarz—have been directed by Mack Bolan to put down terrorist outrages too volatile and unpredictable for regular law enforcement. Able Team works undercover, with deadly purpose, against the most extreme rampages of justice.

THE HOSTAGED ISLAND tells the story of Catalina Island's darkest day, when the rich playground off the coast of Los Angeles is host to more than seventy filthy motorcycle hoodlums. They take over the island in a violent conspiracy cooked up by a Soviet double-agent. Gasoline in the sprinkler system of the Casino's ballroom turns the entire building into a bomb. Only Able Team can neutralize such a menace, and each member gets to play a crucial part. Here is Blancanales in action:

Footprints appeared on the cow trail. Blancanales stopped for a second to check the tracks. Going on, he saw more and more footprints—jogging shoes, hiking boots, sandals. The bubble-gum wrappers and cigarette butts and empty cans indicated frequent visitors.

At first, he thought the sounds were gull cries from the ocean. He listened harder. It was laughter, coarse laughter, coming from the campground.

Unsnapping the flap of his Browning Double-Action holster, he slipped out the pistol. Then he changed his mind. He found the Beretta 93R in his backpack, slapped in a magazine and snapped back the slide.

Soft-footing it along the trail, crouching below the level of the brush, he could hear screams, more laughter, voices. He continued another hundred yards. He couldn't go any farther without losing cover. But another scream told him he was already there. Fifty yards below him, two Outlaws raped a woman. One struggled on top of her. The other biker stood on her arms, urging his cohort on, taunting him.

Sliding and crawling as fast as he dared through the thick sagebrush, Blancanales silently closed the distance between himself and the bikers. Twenty yards on, he lay prone in the brush. His hands extended from cover, grasping the Beretta. His right hand was on the grip, his left hand held the extension lever in front of the trigger guard, left thumb through the extra-large trigger guard. He sighted on the standing biker's chest and gave him a three-round burst.

The bullets interrupted a laugh, the first round punching into the biker's chest, the second his collarbone, the third taking away his left eye and sideburn. He fell backward and thrashed on the gravel.

The woman clawed at the other biker's face and twisted out from under him. She blocked Blancanales' aim. He broke cover, ran and slid and jumped down the hillside. The biker scrambled to his feet, his pants around his knees, trying to pull a pistol from a shoulder holster.

The snap shot glanced off the top of the biker's head, sent him staggering backward. Blancanales finally reached the bottom of the hill, dropped into a two-handed, wide-leg stance to deliver the kill shot, when the woman again blocked his aim as she kicked and punched the bleeding biker.

"Get down!" Blancanales shouted. "Out of the way! Let me kill him!"

She turned and saw him for the first time. Her eyes went wide at the sight of the black-clad warrior with the pistol. But she didn't move. The biker sprinted away, weaving through trees and brush. Blancanales sighted, fired again, heard the bullet slap the biker. He fell, scrambled up, kept running.

Starting after the wounded biker, Blancanales yelled back at the woman: "Take that dead man's weapons, go hide in the brush. Don't show yourself till you see uniformed police officers or soldiers. Move it—I can't help you anymore."

"Thank you, oh, thank you, God be with you," the woman sobbed as Blancanales took chase.

Mack Bolan's
PHOENIX FORCE
AN EXECUTIONER SERIES
by Gar Wilson

Phoenix Force is The Executioner's five-man army that blazes through the dirtiest of encounters. Like commandos who fight for the love of battle and the righteous unfolding of the logic of war, Bolan's five hardasses make mincemeat out of their enemies. Watch for this explosive new series!

"Strong-willed and true. Gold Eagle Books are making history. Full of adventure, daring and action!"
—*Marketing Bestsellers*

#1 Argentine Deadline

On Sale April

Available wherever paperbacks are sold.

GOLD EAGLE